The Chewing-Gum Rescue
and Other Stories

MARGARET MAHY

Eleven exciting new stories by the witty Margaret Mahy. This collection ranges from the hilarious title story to the pure fantasy of *The Travelling Boy and the Stay-at-Home Bird* and *The Devil and the Corner Grocer*.

'Margaret Mahy is incapable of a cliché character, and Jan Ormerod's drawings are a pleasure too.'

The Standard

MARGARET MAHY

The Chewing-Gum Rescue and Other Stories

Illustrated by Jan Ormerod

MAMMOTH

First published 1982 by J. M. Dent & Sons Ltd
Magnet paperback edition published 1984
Reprinted 1984, 1985, 1987 and 1989
Published 1990 by Mammoth
an imprint of Mandarin Paperbacks
Michelin House, 81 Fulham Road, London SW3 6RB
Reprinted 1990 (twice)

Mandarin is an imprint of the Octopus Publishing Group

Text copyright © 1982 Margaret Mahy
Illustrations copyright © 1982 Jan Ormerod

A CIP catalogue record for this title
is available from the British Library

ISBN 0 7497 0250 8

Printed in Great Britain
by Cox & Wyman Ltd, Reading

Contents

The Chewing-Gum Rescue

On the evening of pocket-money day Mr. Frisbee came stumping along to his own back door after shutting up his prize-winning angora goats, Gregorius and Gertrude, for the night. He had been very careful about this for the infamous Gargle Goat Thief Gang was roaming around the countryside, stealing goats of all kinds—very worrying for goat owners. Mr. Frisbee was looking forward to a quiet evening with his wife and children. But as he was wiping his weary feet in their faithful gumboots, suddenly the gumboots stuck to the doormat and he fell head-over-heels into the hall.

'Help! Help!' shouted Mr. Frisbee as he lay there, his feet up in the air and the doormat still stuck to his boots. His five daughters, Florence, Flora, Fenella, Felicity and the baby Francesca came running to see what had happened to their loving father.

'Oh Dad!' cried Florence. 'You have trodden on a piece of Francesca's chewing-gum.'

'Yes,' said Flora. 'You know, Dad! It's on the telly.'

'It's on the doormat too,' grumbled Mr. Frisbee shaking his feet out of their faithful gumboots.

'It's advertised on television,' Flora explained. 'It's Dr. Gumption's simply Great Green Gum with the Daisy Fresh Mint Flavour.'

'It's full of fluoride and chlorophyll and it's the gum that's good for the gums,' said Felicity.

'And it's got champion chewability,' finished Fenella as she helped Felicity pull the doormat away from the gumboots. It took a lot of doing.

'Can't you have ice-cream instead?' asked Mr. Frisbee fretfully.

And Florence, Flora, Felicity, Fenella and even Francesca replied as one daughter, 'Mum won't let us.'

'Of course I won't,' said Mrs. Frisbee firmly, for she was a dentist during the day, and disapproved of sweets and cakes which, as everyone knows, are so bad for children's teeth. 'No ice-creams in this house, no chocolate or sherbert or coconut cream caramels or butterscotch! No fudge or toffee-apples, no brown sugar peanut brittle, and no buttery molasses taffy. Dr. Gumption's Gum is the only thing I'm prepared to tolerate. I want all my daughters to have teeth as strong as tigers' teeth and as beautiful as pearls.'

Well, that very night, after the girls had eaten all their greens, chewed their crusts twenty-five times each and had each finished off with a raw carrot, they sat down to watch television. But no sooner had the television set been switched on than Dr. Gumption himself appeared, smiling and scraping all over the screen.

'Hey kids!' he cried. 'It's good GOOD news. Dr. Gumption has a great new gum on the market and—WOW—its twice as sticky and—mmmmmmmmmm—it's twice as stretchy and—YAY—it's twice as green and it's got double that super duper minty flavour, so listen kids, to what everyone is saying. . . .'

And then a chorus of beautiful girls in green clustered around Dr. Gumption and they sang . . .

'Do friends avoid you? Take the hint!
Chew Dr. Gumption's Minty-mint.'

'Shall we?' Florence signalled to her sisters by wiggling her crooked eyebrows.

'Next pocket-money day!' Flora signalled back with hers.

Next pocket-money day Mr. Frisbee came home after locking up his prize angora goats with tremendous care and he found that the back door wouldn't even open; he had to go round to the front door like a polite visitor. As he came in the smell of minty-mint rolled towards him like a great green ocean.

'What's happened to the back door?' he demanded crossly.

'It's got a piece of Felicity's gum stuck in it,' said Flora, telling tales as she often did.

'Fenella made me put it there,' grumbled Felicity. 'She said . . . "Just for fun put your gum here!" and when I did, she shut the door on it and now we can't get the door open, and my gum has gone for good.'

'Honestly, my dear,' Mr. Frisbee said to his wife, 'a simple orange each would save a lot of trouble in the long run.'

'Never!' declared Mrs. Frisbee (Dentist). 'I spend all day patching up teeth ruined by coconut candy and frosted cakes. Never shall my daughters feast on brandy balls or barley sugar, Turkish delight, marshmallows or chocolate peanuts. They shall have teeth as strong as tigers' teeth and as beautiful as pearls.'

But later, when the lid of the piano refused to open because Francesca's gum was jammed under it, Mrs. Frisbee looked very thoughtful and still later, when the tablecloth stuck to the

9

table just as if it had been nailed at all four corners, she looked quite cross.

That very night on television the beaming face of Dr. Gumption appeared once more.

'Hey kids, hey!' he shouted. 'Boy oh boy! What news! Dr. Gumption's Gum has been improved yet again. Triple Chewability! Quadruple stretch power. Ten times the stickability! Oh that gloptious Gumption Gum. It's the NOW gum! It's the POW gum! And don't forget, kids, it's got that triple ripple super duper minty-mint flavour.' And the girls in green appeared and sang . . .

'Make your father go all numb!
Chew Dr. Gumption's Gloptious Gum!'

'Shall we?' signalled Florence with her crooked eyebrows.

'Yes, yes, yes!' signalled Flora, Felicity, Fenella, and Francesca.

A week later on pocket-money day Mr. Frisbee came home having shut his precious Gregorius and Gertrude away for the night.

'The Gargle Gang will never get them,' he muttered fiercely to himself. 'But locking up is hard work. I'm longing for a cup of tea.' He stumped up the path in his faithful gumboots but he could not open the back door or the front door either. Most of the windows were sealed shut, too, but at last he found that he could open the bathroom window with a stick, and by standing on an up-ended apple box he was able to somersault into his house.

Inside, the smell of Super Duper Minty-mint was so strong he staggered back clutching his throat. Dr. Gumption's chewing-gum stretched everywhere in an evil green web. It was as if a whole houseful of wicked spiders had been at work for a week. It seized your shoes and stuck them to the floor, it caught your coat and held on to your hair. It was like a super duper minty-mint mad monster from Mars stretching from room to room to room.

'Arrrrh!' cried Mr. Frisbee, as his five daughters and

Mrs. Frisbee came to meet him, climbing nimbly through the sticky maze. 'Couldn't you let them have a liquorice all-sort each instead?' he gasped.

'No, no!' replied Mrs Frisbee. 'I'm a dentist as well as a mother. If you saw the horrors that I see every day—molars molested and melted away by refined sugars—you would understand. Never shall my little ones have peppermint creams or coconut ice, boiled lollies, dolly mixtures, raspberry drops, wine gums, humbugs, jujubes or all-day suckers. My daughters must have teeth as strong as tigers' teeth and as beautiful as pearls.'

'I suppose they must,' said Mr. Frisbee wearily.

At dinner that night the soup tasted of Dr. Gumption's Super Duper Minty-mint Gum. The roast beef, roast potatoes, roast onions, roast parsnips, roast pumpkin and buttered beans all tasted of Dr. Gumption's Super Duper Minty-mint Gum and so did the wholesome apple brown-betty and the raw carrots to finish off with. No one enjoyed anything very much.

Yet that very night on television Dr. Gumption appeared again. 'Hey kids!' he shouted. 'Hey—all you gum chewers out there! Have you tried Dr. Gumption's NEW splendiferous magniferous gum? Such expansion. Such extension! It stretches up and out and every whichever way. It's the fun gum that keeps the household happy and healthy. It sticks so well that it's being used by boat builders as a saltwater glue. And it's got that unutterable, that entirely inexpressible super duper triple ripple more-minty-than-mint flavour. WOW!'

Then the girls in green appeared and sang . . .

'Want to make your teacher squint?
Chew Dr. Gumption's Minty-mint.'

'Next time!' Florence signalled Flora, Felicity, Fenella and Francesca, wiggling her eyebrows in time to the music.

A week later on pocket-money day Mr. Frisbee staggered up to bed coughing and choking and fighting off green tentacles of gum.

11

'Man can triumph over any odds,' he muttered. 'He can get used to anything if he has to.' He was a bit lonely because Mrs. Frisbee was out at a Dental Health Conference.

What Mr. Frisbee did not know was that Florence, Flora, Felicity, Fenella and even Francesca all had packets of Dr. Gumption's New More-minty-than-mint Gum tucked under their pillows. They hadn't started chewing it yet because they had some of the old Triple Minty-mint Gum from last week's pocket-money day to use up first.

As he lay awake, missing Mrs. Frisbee B.D.S., Mr. Frisbee heard strange shufflings and muffled bleats coming from the goat pens. They were not very loud and, had Mrs. Frisbee been at home, he would have been sound asleep and would have missed hearing them altogether. As it was he leaped to his feet and peeped out of the window. What a sight met his eyes!

There were the five dreadful Gargle brothers, leaders of the Gargle Goat Thief Gang, not to mention five of their minions. They were in the actual act of stealing Gregorius and Gertrude, Mr. Frisbee's prize-winning angoras. There was not a moment to be lost.

Wrapping his hands in Mrs. Frisbee's second-best petticoat and seizing a strand of Doctor Gumption's Triple Super Duper Minty-mint Gum that happened to be dangling from the guttering, Mr. Frisbee swung down like Tarzan, a curiously splendid figure in his simulated leopardskin pyjamas, screaming reprimands and reproaches at the villainous goat thieves.

Florence and Flora woke up at once and looked out of the window. What they saw horrified them and they hastened to wake up Felicity, Fenella and even Francesca by way of reinforcements. Armed only with Dr. Gumption's New More-minty-than-mint Gum, they climbed out of the bathroom window and whisked over to the goat pens.

For there was no doubt that Mr. Frisbee was getting the worst of it.

In his first spectacular swing he had struck Harvey Gargle to the ground and then as he swept majestically back he had struck Ellis Gargle, knocking out his false teeth and seriously bewildering him. But then he himself hit the side of the house very hard and let go the chewing-gum, falling dazed to the ground, an easy prey to the infuriated goat thieves.

Mad Rory Gargle with two minions advanced upon him in a threatening way; Bernard Gargle (with two other minions) picked up his fallen brothers, not forgetting Ellis's false teeth, while Rackham Gargle with the single remaining minion rapidly led Gregorious Goat and his nanny wife, Gertrude, towards a waiting van.

Victory was within the grasp of the nefarious goat thieves. All seemed lost . . .

When, suddenly, with a lion-like roar Florence sprang out at them from the right, biting firmly into a piece of Dr. Gumption's New More-minty-than-mint gum as she did so. Flora bounded in from the left, whooping and hooting like a whole treeful of owls. There was a hearty hullabaloo from Fenella who, chewing her piece of Dr. Gumption's Mintier-than-mint Gum, came up behind Florence, a blood-curdling growl from Felicity leaping out of the chrysanthemums, and squeaks and squeals from Francesca who rose up out of the watering-can.

The goat thieves were entirely taken aback. This unexpected racket and rumpus-bumpus upset them badly.

'Squad . . . breathe OUT!' shouted Florence and the daughters of the house breathed out as one combined daughter. A terrible wave of unutterable, indescribable, inexpressible, super duper triple ripple more-minty-than-mint aroma swept over the goat thieves.

'Enemy Mint Gas Attack!' shouted Mad Rory Gargle before he dropped like a stone. Lewis and Rackham Gargle and the assorted minions keeled over like slender reeds in a hurricane and even the goats fell to their knees gasping.

Mr. Frisbee, however, had been exposed to Dr. Gumption's punishing mint flavour for at least three weeks and although somewhat unsteady, he was not totally overcome. He had built up an immunity.

'Tie them up!' he ordered. 'Quickly.'

His devoted daughters did not hesitate. Within a moment

the Gargle Gang were wound around with Dr. Gumption's powerful product. The music died down and the goats began to revive. At this very moment Mrs. Frisbee drove the family car into the yard. She was astonished to find it filled with disabled goat thieves, groggy goats, her husband bruised but resplendent in his simulated leopardskin pyjamas, not to mention her five daughters still up well beyond their bedtime.

'You see how wise I was,' she said. 'You couldn't have saved Gregorius and Gertrude with a piece of Turkish delight.'

'I'll never say anything against Dr. Gumption's Mintier-than-mint Gum again,' Mr. Frisbee vowed fervently.

Florence looked at her sisters. 'Shall I tell him?' she signalled with her crooked eyebrows.

'O.K.,' they all signalled back.

'Actually Dad,' said Florence, 'we're getting rather sick of it.'

'Well, that's all right, my dear,' said Mrs. Frisbee quickly, 'because I heard of a delicious new sweet at the Conference today. Honey Bliss it's called and it's made with pure golden honey collected from lime blossoms by particularly happy and busy bees. Of course you'll still have to brush your teeth after it, but you have to do that anyway.'

Florence, Flora, Felicity, Fenella and Francesca looked delighted to hear this. They had enjoyed Dr. Gumption's Gum but it was very hard work keeping it under control and they needed a rest.

The police came and took the goat thieves away. 'We've been waiting a long time to get our hands on this lot,' the Chief Constable said. 'There's a big reward, you know. You'll be able to extend your herd of angora goats.'

Mr. Frisbee, though bruised and battered, beamed with joy.

Shortly after this Dr. Gumption's Gum was withdrawn from the market and only used again in army exercises. Florence, Flora, Felicity, Fenella and Francesca settled down with Honey Bliss which smelt deliciously of lime blossom and tasted wonderful. However, it must be noted that when Gertrude the

14

goat had two beautiful kids a short time later they did have, very faintly, a mintier-than-mint perfume, no doubt due to their mother's exposure to Dr. Gumption's Gum during the great mintier-than-mint goat rescue and the heroic victory of the Frisbee sisters, all of whom grew up to have teeth as strong as tigers' teeth and as beautiful as pearls.

The Giant's Bath

1 *A House with Certain Drawbacks*

Mr. Sweetbriar, the dashing young accountant, had made
quite a lot of money giving good advice to people about income
tax. Day after day you could see troubled people come to his
office weeping and swearing and then departing, after an hour's
refreshing discussion, laughing for joy and pressing money into
Mr. Sweetbriar's hand.

'Dearest,' said Mr. Sweetbriar to his wife, Mrs. Sweetbriar,
'we'll be able to buy a house at last and have a garden like the
one my old granny used to have. Have I ever told you about it?'

'You have mentioned it a few times,' said Mrs. Sweetbriar,
smiling. 'It was full of lavender bushes and rose trees, wasn't
it?'

'It had a herb garden and hollyhocks, too,' Mr. Sweetbriar
cried. 'We'll have a garden just like that one.'

Mrs. Sweetbriar and the twins Belinda and Melinda were
very excited.

'I'll have room to practise my archery,' Mrs. Sweetbriar
rejoiced, for she had been Ladies Longbow Champion for five
years running, and had actually met Mr. Sweetbriar by accidentally shooting off his hat one day in the Botanical Gardens.

'And we'll have room for a tree-house!' Melinda and
Belinda cried happily, for climbing trees was their hobby, and
they spent as much time as they could up among the leaves of
the tallest trees in town.

But you know how it is—it isn't easy to find the exact house
that suits you. The Sweetbriars looked at dozens, but some
houses were too rich—all marble staircases and grand
pianos—and others were too poor, all empty mouse-holes and
deserted cobwebs.

'Don't despair!' said Mr. Sweetbriar nobly. And they

didn't despair but kept on looking until the estate agent found them a house that very nearly suited them all.

It had a long lawn, highly suitable for archery, many fine trees that could easily support a whole village of tree-houses in their spreading branches, and there were corners and crannies where a garden might be planted.

'I can easily plant a garden,' said Mr. Sweetbriar, 'and build a tree-house or two—simple for any man used to dealing with the intricacies of income tax . . . but there must be some drawback. There's always a drawback.' And he looked sternly at the estate agent.

'Well, there is *one*,' the estate agent confessed. 'You see, this house used to belong to a giant, and it's still got a giant's bathroom. All the other rooms have been divided up man-sized, but we couldn't divide that bathroom. It's because of the giant plumbing, you know. All the pipes and S-bends and so on are giant-sized and don't fit in with the city drains. They belong to the MAGICS system.'

'Magic?' Belinda and Melinda opened their eyes first, and their mouths immediately after.

'MAGICS!' corrected the estate agent. 'It stands for Magician's and Giant's Inundation Conduit System. Would you like to see the bathroom now?'

The bathroom was as big as a dance hall and the bath was like a swimming pool, gleaming white and bath-shaped, but enormous. It was built alongside the wall with an attractive surround of greenish-blue tiles with pink-and-white waterlilies painted on them. Beside the bath was a recessed soap-dish, big enough to hold a bubble car, containing a vast cake of rainbow-coloured giant's soap.

'It *is* very big,' said Mr. Sweetbriar doubtfully, after inspecting these generous facilities.

'And very cheap!' said the estate agent, looking at the ceiling high above them.

'It *is* very cheap,' agreed Mrs. Sweetbriar, thinking of the long lawn so suitable for archery, and giving Mr. Sweetbriar an encouraging nudge.

'You see, people like the view,' the agent said, 'and they like the neighbourhood, and they like the lawn and the trees, but they're terrified of the bathroom. It gives them the willies. I think it's the look of the plughole.'

The plughole rather gave Mr. Sweetbriar the willies too, but he didn't like to admit it.

'Do you think if we all took our baths together it mightn't seem so big?' he asked Mrs. Sweetbriar.

'I'm sure we could manage,' Mrs. Sweetbriar replied. 'There's more than a year's supply of soap there, for one thing.'

'And we can both swim dog-paddle,' Belinda and Melinda reminded their hesitant father.

So Mr. Sweetbriar bought the house, plughole, MAGICS plumbing system and all. The Sweetbriar family moved in the following Saturday and began to have baths in the giant's bath almost at once.

2 *Splashing around in the Giant's Bath*

Once they got used to it the Sweetbriars found the giant's bath a lot of fun. It was impossible not to enjoy such warm, deep water at the end of a tiring day. Of course the twins could dog-paddle, but just to be on the safe side Mr. Sweetbriar bought them rubber rings—red for Belinda and blue for Melinda. Every evening, instead of complaining at bath-time the way they used to do, Belinda and Melinda rushed to climb up the ladder on to the end of the bath, and then slid down the long white slope into the translucent depths. Not only this, the giant's soap proved to be full of surprises. Mrs. Sweetbriar cut a little bit off it every night. The first night it made a lovely pink foam that tasted like strawberries, the second time, the bath filled with yellow bubbles as big as pumpkins, and the third night all the bathwater turned to orange juice—rather sticky for bathing in, but delicious if you happened to swallow any accidentally, which frequently happened in the giant's bath.

Then Mr. Sweetbriar discovered a row of three buttons in the side of the giant's bath and these made washing more interesting than ever. For instance, if you pressed the first one a beautiful fountain sprang up in the middle of the bath, leaping almost to the ceiling in a sparkling, silvery plume. If you pressed the second one the fountain went into reverse and a charming little whirlpool appeared, whirling you round and round, chuckling in a soft watery fashion. But it was always best to be getting out of the bath (the Sweetbriars used a rope-ladder for this) before pressing the third button, because a little windlass started up, the monster plug came out of the plughole and the water began to rush out roaring and howling like a tribe of savage hobyahs, terrible to hear. Most plugholes have a little grating inside them which catches toy boats and face flannels, but this one gaped like a black thirsty mouth drinking greedily, never satisfied until the very last drop had been swallowed.

As far as mere washing was concerned the Sweetbriars' new house with its fabulous bath was a great success, but of course there is more to life than washing. Mr. Sweetbriar, for example, in spite of all his good intentions, found he was far too busy to plant a garden like the one his old granny used to have, let alone build a tree-house for the twins. When he should have been out planting catmint, poppies and sweet-william—maybe even a few peppermint pinks—he was doing a lot of work that he had to get finished by Monday. When he should have been out pruning apple trees, he was puzzling over the income tax of artists and musicians, all of whom proved incapable of working it out themselves.

Mrs. Sweetbriar had her problems, too. She was not only expert with a bow and arrow, but she could bake cakes and biscuits to perfection. It would have been nice for her to have some visitors for her cake tins were always full, but somehow or other no neighbours came calling. The neighbours were suspicious of anyone living in the giant's house and preferred to stay at home, watching the Sweetbriars through their curtains. Perhaps, too, they were rather alarmed by seeing Mrs. Sweetbriar

at her archery practice for, armed with her bow and arrows, she seemed a veritable Amazon, fierce and beautiful.

'All right! If they want to keep their distance let them. I don't care,' muttered Mrs. Sweetbriar, but she would have dearly loved some friendly visitors for all that.

She enjoyed conversation, and though Belinda and Melinda had a lot to say it was mostly about tree-houses. They wished their father would hurry up and build them a tree-house, now that they had plenty of trees with suitable branches. Mr. Sweetbriar had bought them a canoe so that they could paddle up and down in the bath, but a canoe is just not the same sort of thing as a tree-house.

One fragrant Friday evening Mr. Sweetbriar came home, his case full of papers to work on over the weekend.

'Hello, my dears, here I am,' he called and Mrs. Sweetbriar called back, 'We're here in the bathroom.'

What a scene of domestic bliss met Mr. Sweetbriar's eyes as he climbed the ladder and joined his wife on the blue-green tiles at the end of the bath. Mrs. Sweetbriar had set out a picnic meal of ham salad, bread rolls, fruit cake, and a bottle of her home-made elderflower champagne. The twins in their canoe, wearing their red and blue rubber rings, were paddling up and down the great bath and using Mrs. Sweetbriar's bow to fire arrows at a small piece of the giant's soap that bobbed obligingly on the surface of the water looking like a foaming pink hedgehog.

'My dear,' Mrs. Sweetbriar exclaimed. 'Here you are at last. Why don't you take off that accounting suit and have a little dip while I toss the salad?'

Mr. Sweetbriar did not entirely like the idea of a little dip while the twins were shooting arrows around with gay abandon. He waved a hand towards them as they pulled arrows out of the piece of giant's soap. 'I hope that's all right,' he remarked in a troubled voice.

'Oh yes, perfectly,' said Mrs. Sweetbriar. 'It's only my third-best bow.'

'That's not what I meant,' Mr. Sweetbriar replied irritably. 'I meant that I hope they shoot straight.'

There was something about his gloomy voice that annoyed the fiery Melinda. 'Daddy—we always shoot straight,' she cried. 'Watch!'

Double-quick as lightning she fitted an arrow to the bow, looked around for a target, found one, aimed and fired. Unfortunately she hit exactly what she was aiming at. Unfortunately she hit the third button in the side of the bath.

Immediately the windlass started, the plug came out and the water began to drain away with a hoarse roar, like a dragon clearing its throat and then gargling. A savage current seized the canoe with Belinda and Melinda, not to mention Mrs. Sweetbriar's third-best bow and a collection of arrows, and swung it towards the gaping plughole. Mrs. Sweetbriar, without a moment's hesitation, flung herself into the bath and struck out after the canoe in a powerful crawl.

Mr. Sweetbriar did wait for a moment (after all he *was* wearing his best accountancy suit and holding an unopened bottle of elderflower champagne) but his hesitation was of the very merest. Still holding the champagne he dived in after his rapidly vanishing family, hoping to assist them in their hour of need. All in vain! The plughole current was fuming and fierce. Hissing like a whip it curled itself around Mr. Sweetbriar, spinning him like a teetotum. The water shrieked in his ears as, shouting and spinning, he was swept into the great, drinking, black mouth of the plughole. Still shouting and spinning he vanished into darkness after Mrs. Sweetbriar and Melinda and Belinda, together with the family canoe, the third-best bow, and the bottle of elderflower champagne.

The plughole took everyone and everything. There was a last fearsome gurgle, then silence fell in the Sweetbriar bathroom.

The giant's bath shone with a pure and arctic whiteness. It was totally empty.

3 *Down the Giant's Drain*

Up bobbed Mr. Sweetbriar almost at once, splittering and spluttering. He was being carried down the giant's drain in a steady rush of water, paddling like a dog, gaping like a frog. It was enough to give a man the willies.

'Where is all this leading?' he thought, but at that very moment a hand seized his soggy collar. Leaning perilously over the edge of the canoe, Belinda held on to him while he struggled aboard and Melinda on the other side pulled Mrs. Sweetbriar to safety. In the bottom of the canoe lay the bow and arrows and the bottle of elderflower champagne which Mr. Sweetbriar had dropped when he dived into the bath. Mr. Sweetbriar was pleased to see it but he felt he ought to grumble a little first, just in case his family thought they could always get away with this sort of thing.

'Little did I think when I was working out Mrs. Fysshe-Freeman's tax return this morning, that I would end the day floating down a giant's drain,' he said in a petulant voice.

'Don't be like that, Daddy. I didn't do it on purpose,' Melinda said coaxingly. 'Besides, this is a MAGICS drain—remember?'

'Magician's and Giant's Inundation Conduit System,' Belinda quoted smiling to herself. 'Isn't it fun?'

'It was getting boring just washing anyway,' Melinda went on. 'It was time for something new to happen.'

A faint luminous glow lit the giant's drain with a greenish radiance. They were travelling so quickly that Mr. Sweetbriar thought they might be floating downhill. But no direction made sense any more in that greenish gloom with the water hurrying them along helter-skelter.

Belinda and Melinda tried to comfort their disgruntled father. 'We're like explorers,' Belinda said. 'Explorers on an unknown underground river. We could wind up anywhere.'

'I don't want to wind up anywhere,' replied Mr. Sweetbriar. 'Where I was, was where I wanted to be. And what's that roaring sound?'

'Lions!' cried Belinda hopefully.

'A waterfall—we're going to go over a waterfall,' hissed Melinda at the same time.

'For goodness sake . . .' Mr. Sweetbriar looked at his wife sternly. 'What are you going to do about this? Are you content just to sit there and go over a waterfall or be eaten by lions?'

'Now, dearest, don't get upset,' said Mrs. Sweetbriar in a very sensible voice. 'You know how the children exaggerate. I don't think it's lions or even a waterfall. I think it's . . .'

Riding triumphantly on a warm wave of bath water, rather squashed together in the canoe, the Sweetbriars shot out of the drain into a river, quiet as velvet in the soft evening.

The roaring sound came from ahead, a slow rolling roar followed by a stormy sigh. It was breakers beating down on the sand. It was the sea, angry and sad turn and turn about, as it fretted at the edge of the land.

The canoe, paddled by Melinda, sidled on down the river and then ran aground on a shelving bank.

'Everyone out!' commanded Mr. Sweetbriar and the whole Sweetbriar family scrambled on to a little beach, a crescent of silver sand. It was as if they had landed on the new moon. Down to the edge of the sand crowded a forest of trees with long slender trunks and tangled branches. Beyond the trees rose steep hills, covered with more trees, tucked in with shadows.

In the very middle of their little beach stood a single tree, its branches touched with the light of a twilight moon. It looked so odd and out of place in the middle of the sand that Mr. Sweetbriar gave it a doubtful look, wondering what it had done to have been pushed away from the others out in the sand on its own.

However, a stray tree was really none of his business. He turned to his family.

'All well so far!' he said. 'No lions! No waterfalls! Now all we've got to do is to find out where we are.'

'Why don't we ask that princess?' Belinda suggested.

'What princess? Where?' asked Mr. Sweetbriar rather snappily.

'The one that looks like a tree,' Belinda said. 'The one on the beach.'

Mr. Sweetbriar peered at the tree in the sand. It did look a little like a person, a branching sort of person watching the sea. He peered again and this time there was no doubt about it. Sitting on a throne of sand, lit by the moonlight reflected from the sea, was a very strange and beautiful princess, watching them out of dark-shaded eyes beneath mossy eyebrows. Her hair flowed like vines of shadow over her shoulders and down her back, entwined with chains of leaves and flowers. Surprisingly, even above the salt-and-seaweed smell of the sea Mr. Sweetbriar thought he smelled the summer garden scent of catmint, reminding him of his old granny's garden—the garden of his childhood.

He glanced around him for a second time, noting the darkness and stillness of the forest and the hills. Then, making up his mind, he walked over the sand towards the princess, followed by his dear family who paused only to collect the bow, the arrows and the elderflower champagne.

Mr. Sweetbriar cleared his throat firmly and spoke to the silent princess.

'Excuse me, Miss—er—that is to say, Your Highness—can you tell me how we can get home?'

The princess looked at him as if she was not at all sure

whether to believe in him—a new experience for Mr. Sweet-briar, for usually everyone believes in accountants. Then she smiled a little.

'I don't think I *can* help you,' she said in a rustling leafy voice. 'I have a lot on my mind right now. At any moment a sea dragon is going to appear out of the sea and devour me. That's what they do, you know. I think you'd be safer up in the trees. I wouldn't trust him not to try tasting someone else after he's finished eating me.'

4 *Dealing with a Dragon*

'You're going to devoured by a dragon?' cried Mr. Sweet-briar. 'But what are you going to do about it?' He refused to let his children watch any violence on television and he thought it would be most unsuitable for them to see a princess devoured by a dragon, even if it swallowed her whole.

'Well, I'm just waiting to be eaten, really,' the princess replied. 'You know how it is . . . a dragon comes along and threatens to burn down the whole kingdom unless he is given a lot of treasure and a beautiful princess. It's been done before, of course—dragons never come up with anything new.'

'What kingdom?' asked Mr. Sweetbriar, glancing around in surprise at the forest and the wooded hills beyond. Where he looked, he could see nothing but trees!

'I'm not a princess in a big way,' the princess explained. 'I'm just princess of this little forest. My subjects are the trees, the birds, and other half-and-half people like myself. We live in tunnels under the roots of the trees or up in the branches in nests and tree-houses.'

'Tree-houses!' cried Melinda and Belinda with one voice.

'But don't wait around,' the princess warned them anxiously. 'The dragon could be here at any moment and I wouldn't put it past him to eat you all if he finds you here. They're not all that particular what they eat.'

'Really!' replied Mr. Sweetbriar rather coldly.

'I mean—they prefer princesses,' the princess explained, 'but they don't insist upon them. Blue blood is optional with dragons.'

'But we can't just leave you around to be eaten. It's horrible,' complained Mr. Sweetbriar. 'You're not tied up, are you? Come away with us. We'll go up the river and try to get back through the giant's drain. All the bath water will have flowed away by now.'

'Yes, but then my kingdom gets burned,' the princess objected. 'No point in being a princess unless you're prepared to get eaten for your country's good. One might just as well be a mere prime minister. Little do you understand how noble a princess has to be to do her job well.'

A very obstinate expression passed over Mr. Sweetbriar's face. Little did the princess realise how persistent an accountant can be in his client's interests.

'Well, I simply refuse to leave you here,' he said. 'If you stay, I stay!' In spite of wearing a wet suit and looking rather out of place talking to a princess on a deserted silver beach, Mr. Sweetbriar actually managed to appear just as heroic as the princess—indeed, more so. Then he turned to his wife and children.

'My dears, climb the nearest tall tree as quickly as you can. Don't fear for me. Remember I have a degree in Commercial Law and anyone who can argue with the income tax department can certainly take on a mere dragon.'

At this moment the sea, always restless and curling, began to toss and spiral in a most disquieting manner.

'What's that!' cried Mr. Sweetbriar in alarm.

'It's the dragon arriving, I'm afraid,' answered the princess calmly. 'Do please hide while there is time.'

'Thank goodness! I thought for a moment someone had pulled the plug out of the sea.' Mr. Sweetbriar sighed with relief. 'We've just had rather a nasty experience with a plughole and it's left me a bit on the jumpy side. But it doesn't weaken my resolve.'

He turned to see Belinda and Melinda, more at home in a tree than on solid earth, helping Mrs. Sweetbriar into the difficult lower branches of a particularly tall one. They soon had her concealed among the leaves and quite invisible to any dragon who might appear out of the surging waves. Mr. Sweetbriar was glad they were safely hidden, but he couldn't help feeling a little bit lonely on that silver beach watching the water swirl and boil.

As the moon danced and splintered and danced again, the dragon's lumpy snout came up through the very centre of the moon's reflection and was followed by no less than three malevolent eyes—the right one red, the left one green and the one directly over the snout bright yellow. Mr. Sweetbriar was immediately reminded of traffic-lights and he couldn't help grinning a bit, a grin which the dragon noticed and immediately resented.

'Ha! Supper!' cried the dragon in a scrunching voice. 'Hello, Princess Snack! And who's this little appetizer?'

'Now look here . . .' began Mr. Sweetbriar, but the dragon ignored him.

'You've got the treasure, of course,' it snarled.

'It's here at my feet,' the princess said, and Mr. Sweetbriar stared, fascinated, at a little pile of treasure suddenly painted in by moonbeams . . . silver goblets, chains of gold, coins, and rings with sapphires and emeralds. 'But don't eat this man here!' the princess pleaded. 'He's nothing to do with the forest or the treasure. He hasn't any blue blood. He's just incidental.'

'A very delicious-looking little incident, for all that!' the dragon said, coming further out of the sea. 'I'll eat anyone I fancy, and he looks a very crunchy little fellow.'

Mr. Sweetbriar, even in the stress of the moment, was charmed to notice that the dragon appeared to be a bright sky-blue on his back, shoulders and tail, deepening to a rich navy at the tips of his spikes and spines, whereas his chest and stomach were the delicate blush-pink of early sunrise.

But 'handsome is as handsome does' is a good rule to bear in mind where dragons are concerned.

'In fact I'll *start* with him,' the dragon said and opened a mouth that made Mr. Sweetbriar think of a cave fringed with stalactites and stalagmites and carpeted with a long blue tongue.

'Now look here,' Mr. Sweetbriar began nervously, 'I have a degree in Commercial Law . . .'

'Big deal!' interrupted the dragon rudely. 'I don't suppose it will spoil the way you taste.' He was just moving in on Mr. Sweetbriar when there came a sharp musical twang and an arrow hit the dragon right in the centre of his pink chest.

'Oh, trying to be smart, are you?' cried the dragon, astonished at first but becoming increasingly testy. 'All right—I'll eat you, then the princess. Then I'll burn the forest, and finally I'll steal the treasure. You've really got my goat this time, and I intend to show you that a dragon's goat is not to be got.'

Another arrow pinged in beside the first. It was really superb marksmanship. You could tell at once that the arm and eye of a longbow champion were directing those arrows. Unfortunately the dragon was very large and the arrows did not go in very far.

'Stop it!' the dragon yelled. 'Stop it, I say!' Then suddenly he let out a terrible yammering yell. 'Ahhhhhhhhhh! I'm poisoned! I'm poisoned. You've polluted the arrows with gall and wormwood. I'm toxicologised! Ahhhhhhh! I'm dying, dying young. I'm only two thousand years old and now I've had it! I'm fading in the flower of my youth.' This was true. Before their very eyes the dragon's sky-blue was fading to a dirty grey, and the lovely pink of his chest, which had shone so rosily in the moonlight, turned to a horrible mottled orange. The dragon collapsed in the shallow water, waving his paws feebly, whining and complaining in a very cowardly fashion.

The princess looked at Mr. Sweetbriar curiously and even a little disapprovingly, which seemed hardly fair. For his part, Mr. Sweetbriar contented himself with shrugging in an offhand way, and tried to conceal his own astonishment.

The princess turned to the dragon again. 'Are you sure?' she asked curiously.

'Of course I'm sure,' the dragon moaned. 'He's tipped the arrows with some toxin . . . goblin grease, or giant's soap or something. No doubt about it, I've had it now.' He flapped around, looking very pathetic in the shallow water at the edge of the sea.

'Giant's soap?' exclaimed Mr. Sweetbriar in astonishment. 'I suppose there just might be a trace of giant's soap on the end of those arrows. You see, before we were sucked down the drain, my daughters Belinda and Melinda were—but I won't go into that now. *I* didn't know that giant's soap was poisonous.'

'Only to dragons,' murmured the dragon weakly, watching the princess as she stepped down from her throne of sand. 'It's not the sort of thing you would know. But giant's soap causes instant atrophy in dragons.'

'I'm afraid there's nothing we can do for you,' the princess said, rather regretfully, which was very sporting of her in the circumstances.

'No! No!' agreed the dragon feebly. 'This is IT! I'm going to snuff it. The only thing that could just possibly faintly save me is an anecdote.'

'You mean antidote,' Mr. Sweetbriar corrected him.

'Don't you go sticking your nose in, making my last hour miserable with pedantic scholarship!' hissed the dragon. 'Antidote or anecdote, it's all the same thing, when there isn't any of it.'

'Any of what?' asked the princess curiously.

'Elderberry wine— that's what!' the dragon sighed. 'That's all that could possibly save me now.'

'I'm sorry I haven't got any,' said the princess.

Mr. Sweetbriar felt someone give a tug at the coat of his damp accounting suit. Mrs. Sweetbriar, Belinda and Melinda had scrambled down out of their tree and come up quietly behind him.

'Daddy! Daddy!' cried Belinda and Melinda together (but with Belinda about two words ahead of Melinda). 'What about

30

that bottle of wine that got washed down the drain with us?'

'Ahem!' said Mr. Sweetbriar in a modest voice. 'I was just coming to that.' (He did not like to confess that he had forgotten about it entirely.) He turned to the dragon again. 'Would a sup of elderflower champagne be likely to have any therapeutic effect?'

The dragon opened its traffic-light eyes a chink. 'It might,' it said cautiously. 'I'll just try a spoonful, if there is any lying around.'

'By a strange coincidence—or possibly the decree of fate—I happen to have a bottle of elderflower champagne on me,' Mr. Sweetbriar said. 'I don't normally carry it around, but . . .'

'Give it to me! Give it to me!' shrieked the dragon in such a hysterical fashion that Belinda and Melinda, who were both particularly brave, looked at him scornfully.

'Well, I will,' said Mr. Sweetbriar, 'but first you've got to promise . . .'

'Is this a time for pettifogging conditions?' whined the dragon. 'I could go at any moment, and I'm an endangered species, too.'

'I think it's just the time for conditions,' Mr. Sweetbriar said firmly. 'You've got to promise to behave in future.'

'Yes,' cried the princess. 'You've got to swear by the great Sea Dragons of the Atlantic and the Pacific and the little red dragon of the Indian Ocean, not to mention the ancient white dragons of the North Pole and the South Pole, not to burn my forest or eat me up or steal my treasure.'

'I might as well die then,' mumbled the dragon sulkily. 'What's the use of surviving when life's going to be so boring from now on?'

'Oh well, it's your decision,' said the princess, turning away as if she was getting rather bored too.

But the dragon, who by now had turned a leaden grey all over, flapped feebly and cried, 'I promise! I promise by all the great dragons to do all the things you said. Let me try some elderflower champagne and I'll live on kippers and kelp for the rest of my born days.'

The cork flew off the elderflower champagne with a festive 'pop' and foamed merrily in the moonlight into a silver goblet the princess produced from the little pile of treasure around her throne. Mrs. Sweetbriar and Belinda and Melinda lifted the dragon's heavy, spiky head so that it could lap weakly at the champagne with its long blue tongue. Like a rare morning dawning in the east, its chest and belly began to flush faintly. Streaks of rosy pink spread through its scales again, while a pure sky-blue crept over the dragon's back and shoulders.

'I feel life returning to me,' sighed the dragon. 'Oh the relief! Give me more! It's very good!'

'It's a recipe of my old granny's,' Mr. Sweetbriar said proudly.

'*I* made it,' added Mrs. Sweetbriar, who was a bit tired of Mr. Sweetbriar's old granny and her many virtues.

'It's better than common elderberry wine,' the dragon cried. 'I feel a new dragon. I blush for my behaviour in the recent past.' And he did too. His chest turned scarlet and his back and shoulders purple, while his spikes and spines deepened to a rich indigo.

'Things aren't too easy for dragons these days,' he continued. 'I mean, you get a bit of treasure saved up through dedication and hard work—the merest keg or two of diamonds, a trumpery coffer of emeralds, a few fiddle-faddle rubies tossed into a miniscule bag of chamois leather—nothing much when you take the time and trouble into consideration—and the next minute you have an income tax assessor with a hat and polished shoes climbing up the cliff and into your cave without a by-your-leave or thank-you. Well, I ask you! The income tax these days is something cruel for dragons.'

Mr. Sweetbriar stiffened like an old war-horse hearing distant martial music. 'Income tax!' he said slowly. 'Are you having problems?'

'That's what I'm telling you,' said the dragon. 'Honestly, I have enough trouble understanding the forms, let alone filling them in.'

'Why don't you eat the income tax inspectors?' asked Melinda curiously.

The dragon looked at her, and then closed his traffic-light eyes in a very dignified way. 'I don't fancy them,' he said.

'By a strange coincidence,' Mr. Sweetbriar began, 'I am just the person to advise you. Do you use your cave as an office or place of business? You can get an exemption for that, you know. And what about your working expenses . . .'

'Well, I don't know,' the dragon said, looking startled. 'I hadn't thought . . .' Mr. Sweetbriar began to hiss with exasperation.

'Oh dear!' Mrs. Sweetbriar sighed to the princess. 'I don't know how to stop him when he starts talking about income tax.'

But the princess took, from her pile of treasure, a little silver pipe and played three notes so sweet and wild that even Mr. Sweetbriar's flow of commercial advice faltered for a moment. The forest sighed and swayed as if a wind had blown over it yet the air was still, and the sea murmured as if a crowd of people were turning over in their sleep.

5 *Everyone Enjoys Themselves*

Out of the forest came a procession of people as strange and mixed as the princess herself—girls with long leafy hair streaming around them like the trailing pennants of weeping willow, men with antlers like red deer, and owls with eyes so round and golden they looked like coins stolen from the treasure of the woods.

'The treasure is saved, the forest is safe and your princess is still your princess,' the princess told her subjects. 'Therefore I declare this to be party-time.'

Someone began to play on a pipe, a leafy girl struck up on a green violin, bush rats beat on drums no bigger than walnuts. A spiky child with purple eyes offered a bowl of blackberries. A boy glittering with golden dust and wearing a strange, furry mask offered round the honey of wild bees, still in its waxy comb. Out of the sea came a lot of mermaids who liked honey but didn't very often get a chance to taste any, and joined in the party. All the time, at the edge of the sea, just where the little frilly waves curled and broke into foam the dragon and Mr. Sweetbriar talked earnestly, Mr. Sweetbriar making an occasional note in his still damp pocket-book.

'I think you should look hard at the possibility of becoming a limited liability company,' Mrs. Sweetbriar heard her husband saying as she danced by. She smiled and lifted her face to the sky and saw that it was beginning to be morning.

Slowly the people of the forest began to vanish back into the shadows just under the trees. Slowly the mermaids let their webbed fingers uncurl from the rocks and drifted back under the waves.

Belinda and Melinda came scrambling down out of the trees, where they had been swaying and singing. Now they were smiling and yawning. The beach that had whirled with dancers and musicians all night was now empty except for the Sweetbriars, the dragon, the princess and a thousand strange footsteps which the tide was already wiping away. Belinda yawned again and the dragon yawned, too.

'Is it morning already?' he asked. 'How time has flown. Would you like a lift home? It'll save you having to struggle back up the giant's drain, carrying the canoe.'

'That would be very nice,' said Mrs. Sweetbriar quickly. 'The girls are tired out. Good morning, Princess, and thank you for a lovely party. I'm so glad we were able to make ourselves useful.'

'We'll meet again soon,' said the princess. 'After all, now you know the way, and so do we.'

The dragon was so covered with spikes and spines that it wasn't altogether easy to find a comfortable spot, particularly when the canoe had to be fitted on, too. Fortunately the journey was not long, and being rather uncomfortable was an advantage because nobody went to sleep. The dragon went up in a simple spiral into the pink morning clouds and in no time at all was gliding down on to the Sweetbriars' lawn. Mrs. Sweetbriar was sure she saw the curtains twitch at the window of the left-hand house, where a very gossipy old retired company director lived with seven cats and forty-two goldfish.

'Oh well, that's that,' she thought. 'Bad enough having a giant's bath in the house. Now they've seen us coming home by dragon they'll never ever come visiting and try my apple-sauce cake. But who cares! We've had a lovely party, an exciting adventure—and we've been useful to the princess AND the dragon. You can't have everything in this life and we've got more than most.'

With these philosophical thoughts she helped the twins out of their rubber rings, which had become air-supports as well. Did she but know, however, the adventure of the giant's bath was not over yet.

6 Gardens, Tree-houses and Visitors

On Monday as usual Mr. Sweetbriar parked his car in the family drive and walked up the dim shadowy path that led to his house. Silver birches rustled mysteriously. Mr. Sweetbriar hesitated, sniffed, looked around, peering through the dusk.

Catmint! There was definitely the smell of catmint in the air. As he stood, puzzled, he heard someone laugh softly and the tinkle of little golden bells. Light streaming from the windows lit up a few nooks and crannies beside the stone steps. A garden had suddenly blossomed. Creeping roses scrambled over the old stones. Poppies and daisies grew in radiant clumps. Mr. Sweetbriar bent towards them, thinking he could also see snapdragons and candytuft. The golden bells tinkled again and someone moved under the trees. The garden was alive with secret movement.

After a hard day's work the scent of catmint and roses lifted Mr. Sweetbriar's flagging spirits. Income tax seemed no more than an uneasy dream. He didn't waste time looking for people

who didn't want to be looked at. Instead he fairly bounded u[p]
the steps and through his own front door.

'I'm home!' he called cheerfully. 'Here I am! What's fo[r]
dinner?'

'We're all in the bathroom,' called Mrs. Sweetbriar.

'Where else?' thought Mr. Sweetbriar as he skipped along
to this well-loved room.

What a scene met his astonished eyes!

On the tiled end of the bath stood Mrs. Sweetbriar, elegan[t]
in her black hostess skirt and sparkly top, setting out plates o[f]
cakes, pikelets with jam and cream, and special biscuits calle[d]
walnut-fudge-follies.

'Daddy!' Belinda called. 'Daddy, the princess has bee[n]
here with a lot of other foresty people and they've planted [a]
garden and made us tree-houses.'

'Mine's in the chestnut tree,' Melinda added.

'Mine's in the plum tree,' said Belinda, swinging from th[e]
rope-ladder.

Mr. Sweetbriar smiled at his twins fondly.

'Well, my dear,' he said to his wife, 'what sort of day hav[e]
you had?'

'Archery all morning,' Mrs. Sweetbriar replied, 'and visi[-]
tors all afternoon. Come and meet them.'

'Where?' said Mr. Sweetbriar bewildered.

There came the sound of splashing and singing from th[e]
bath. Mr. Sweetbriar climbed the ladder and looked down.

The giant's bath was full of mermaids. They waved at hi[m]
and laughed, making a noise like tinkling bells.

'Everyone came up the drain,' Mrs. Sweetbriar said. 'I wa[s]
quite taken aback. Fortunately all my cake-tins were full. The[y]
just love the walnut-fudge-follies. There's honey in those, yo[u]
know, and mermaids really enjoy honey. Oh I feel so happy[.]
Do you mind not having a bath tonight since we have so man[y]
visitors?'

'I feel a little tired for washing tonight anyway,' Mr. Sweet[-]
briar said gallantly. 'I've spent the whole day trying to do th[e]
dragon's income tax return and believe me, it is so complicate[d]

36

that I'm worn out. But it is rewarding work. I don't think an endangered species ought to be taxed so heavily, do you?'

'Certainly not!' said Mrs. Sweetbriar.

Mr. Sweetbriar took a walnut-fudge-folly and a glass of elderflower champagne and looked around contentedly. The great room was silvered with wisps of steam, foaming strawberry-pink with giant's soap, merry with the laughter of mermaids and the giggling of the twins.

Turning to Mrs. Sweetbriar he said, 'You know, my dear, I feel quite sorry for those who don't have a giant's bath in the family.'

The Midnight Story on Griffon Hill

Martin and Micky Ingoldsby loved swimming. They could do back stroke, breast stroke, and butterfly. They could do dog paddle, duck paddle and Australian crawl. All who saw them in the school swimming pool were heard to remark, 'Those boys are natural swimmers.'

'Yes,' their sports teacher would say, 'and it's really amazing because they spend most of their time looking after their father, and don't get a chance to do much swimming at all—just a little bit during the lunch hour at school.'

Martin and Micky dreamed of water and swimming, of green rivers and blue oceans, of glassy pools and sparkling lakes. However, they seldom managed to visit the seaside or the riverside or the lakeside because their father was always too busy to take them.

They lived with their industrious parent in a tall house surrounded by a tangly garden at the foot of Griffon Hill—one of those alarming bony hills with wild paths leading nowhere, fierce rocks, and the feeling of having an ancient secret held in its dark heart. Griffons had once lived in the caves and caverns of Griffon Hill and sometimes it seemed that the air still throbbed with the beat of their great eaglish wings and echoed with their lionish cries. If you were lucky you might find a fossilized griffon feather or griffon's paw-mark, and at the back gate of the Ingoldsby house was a big stony pit where men had once dug for the griffon's treasure, without ever finding it. It was said that the last of the griffons had wept a fortune in pearls, but if it was true there was no proof of it. The pearls had gone forever. Although it was strange and lonely, Martin and Micky loved living by mysterious Griffon Hill in the heart of a tangly garden, but they did wish there was some place close at hand where they could practise their swimming. They liked the thought of being champions.

Mr Ingoldsby, their father, was a famous author and his speciality was fun. On Monday he wrote spritely stories and farcical fiction for a family magazine. On Tuesday he would type a laughable legend for the local radio. On Wednesday he would dash off a merry memoir for the *Weekly Wonder*, while on Thursday he wrote some humorous history for the *Evening Egghead*, and on Friday he'd concoct a comical chronicle for the *Householders', Ratepayers' and Pennypinchers' Advertiser*.

His stories were so funny that doctors gave them to people suffering from dejections, doldrums or despondency or even to those who were merely down in the dumps. As the patients read his stories they would begin to simper and smile; they would grin and giggle and guffaw, and at last they would laugh loud and long until they were light-hearted again. Then, when they left the doctor's surgery, they would run straight off to the library to borrow more of these marvellous stories collected in books—they kept melancholy at bay so very successfully.

The trouble was that being funny the whole time, though very good for other people, was very bad for Mr. Ingoldsby. It put him all out of balance. There were times when he longed to write a quiet story or even a sad one. Sometimes it seemed to him that underneath all the chuckling and chortling in his books he could hear the sound of someone weeping, silently and secretly, a mysterious weeping that no one else seemed to notice. Being perpetually humorous made him very bad-tempered, and the funnier he was in his books the crosser he was at home. It wasn't much fun for Martin and Micky living with such a crabby father. Of course they could read his books to remind themselves how nice he could be, but it wasn't as good as if he'd been cheerful with them in the first place.

Every weekend Mr. Ingoldsby was busy with typing, checking, putting in the full-stops that had tried to escape and so on. It wasn't work he enjoyed, and one particular weekend he had only just begun to do it, and was already having trouble with an unruly comma, when there came a knock on his door.

'Go away!' he shouted. However, the knocking came again, quiet but very determined. Mr. Ingoldsby threw a slipper at the door in a fretful way, but the door took no notice and actually opened a little bit. Martin looked cautiously in, just above the door-handle, and Micky looked nervously in just below it.

'What do you want?' cried Mr. Ingoldsby. 'You know I'm busy.'

'Dad, we've made the beds and we've vacuumed the house,' Martin said.

'So what!' shouted his irascible parent.

'We've swept the cobwebs and frightened the spiders,' squeaked Micky.

'Big deal!' growled Mr. Ingoldsby, still thinking of that wretched comma.

'We've done the dishes and wiped the bench and hung out the washing, and ironed the handkerchiefs and polished the sideboard, the silver and the shoes,' said Martin, 'and now we'd love to go swimming. Summer's almost over and soon it will be too cold for us to enjoy swimming until next spring.'

'Please take us!' Micky begged. 'Last year I could swim like a fish but now I'm almost back to a mere dog paddle. I'm forgetting how to dive. I'm almost forgetting how to get wet. Please, Dad!'

'You want *me* to take you . . . *me*, with all my work!' exclaimed Mr. Ingoldsby. 'Look at it . . . Friday's comical chronicle and Tuesday's laughable legend still full of spelling mistakes, and commas thinking they can do anything they like. I'm up to HERE with work,' cried Mr. Ingoldsby holding his hand well over his head and working himself into an enjoyable fury, 'and if I don't get it done, well, you know what! Bills mounting up. Empty money-boxes, bank balance collapsing. Calamity! Catastrophe!—And that's not counting the poor suffering mortals in the outside world who won't have anything to laugh at! There'll be outbreaks of glumness, I tell you, epidemics of depression. The country will sink beneath waves of gloom, and you'll be the ones to blame, with your selfish demands for swimming and salt water. It's just as well someone's got some sense of responsibility around here. Now get out and leave me to work.'

Martin sighed, but Micky couldn't help shouting back, 'We cook your dinner and clean your shoes but you don't take us anywhere. You're mean. You're only nice in books, never ever in real life.'

Martin pulled Micky away, just before Mr. Ingoldsby threw his second slipper at them, hitting the wall exactly where Micky's nose had been only a moment before. They ran off, disappointed and disconsolate, and Mr. Ingoldsby, after a bit of snarling, returned to his comical chronicle. But somehow or other he had lost interest in that tricky comma. He left it sitting in the wrong place and sat back pondering gloomily.

'I should have taken the boys swimming,' he thought, 'I'm a terrible father. If only I could tell them how sick of it I am . . . all this ha! ha! ha! and ho! ho! ho! If only they knew that I'm saving to build a little swimming pool in our own back garden as a splendid surprise. But if I told them it wouldn't be a surprise any more. And I'm not even sure I'm going to be able to afford it anyway—not unless I finish these two humorous histories. Oh, it's more than I can bear!'

And he snatched up his pen and began work at once on an entirely new story, a sad story, a story like a lonely song sung on a day of grey slanting rain and falling leaves. There wasn't a laugh in it from beginning to end for it told of the death of the griffons and the downfall of the good giants. It told of the wizards growing old and forgetting their spells of kindness, wandering off down the rough roads of the world on bruised and bleeding feet, of flying horses shot down with arrows, of griffons' eggs growing cold in forgotten caves and little griffons dying in their chilly shells. No one came any longer to rescue the princesses. They died too, alone in ancient towers, and birds made nests out of their shining hair.

As he wrote, tears like commas of glass ran down Mr. Ingoldsby's nose and plopped on to his paper, which was soon punctuated with blisters of wetness.

Late in the afternoon, when he had finished his first and

41

only melancholy tale, he blotted his eyes and his nose and spoke sternly to himself.

'Who would want to read this? There's enough sadness in the world already. Don't get carried away by melancholy, Allardyce Ingoldsby.' So saying he opened his window and looked out on the steep, secret slopes of Griffon Hill where the wind was turning cartwheels all the way from its rocky crest down into the tangles of Mr. Ingoldsby's own garden, spinning like a cog in the year's machinery which was pushing the world on towards autumn, winter and then spring again. The wind built itself towers of late-summer leaves, a whole rustling city of castles, which it let fall away through its careless hands. It turned the trees into harps and ran its fingers through the green hair of the grass. Mr. Ingoldsby watched it and, smiling sadly, posted the pages of his story one by one out of the window.

'No one would have wanted to read it anyway,' he mumbled, watching the wind trundle it, page by page, over the ground and then whirl it like a flight of crumpled birds high against the dark cone of Griffon Hill.

Mr. Ingoldsby padded out to the kitchen. 'I'm sorry I was so cross,' he said to his sons. 'I didn't mean to be like that. We'll go swimming now if you like.'

'It's late,' Martin said. 'Too late . . . look at the long shadows.'

'Look at the clock!' said Micky. 'It's potato-peeling, carrot-scraping time.'

'First thing tomorrow!' Mr. Ingoldsby promised. 'We'll go absolutely first thing tomorrow. Let's get up really early.'

Late that night just as Mr. Ingoldsby was getting into bed something tapped at his window. At first he thought a long white face was looking in at him, but then he saw it was a page of typing paper plastered flat against the glass.

'I weep for the death of griffons, those noble beasts of the world's morning,' he read. It was the first page of his story. It clung there for a moment, and then the night took it back again. It was like a lonely white moth fluttering away.

'What sort of father am I?' wondered Mr. Ingoldsby, feel-

42

ing sorry for his poor crumpled story. 'I'm not very nice to my boys, and I throw my sad stories away because they don't match the funny ones that went before. And after all, *I* liked it, even if no one else did. Perhaps I'll just go and see if it's still blowing around in the garden, and take another look at it.'

He put on his tartan dressing-gown, took Micky's butterfly net and set off into the warm and windy night, under a sky as clear as deep blue glass, all shiny with the light of a full moon.

Mr. Ingoldsby thought he saw the page of his story flapping ahead of him, like a ghost with corners. He lifted the skirts of his tartan dressing-gown with one hand and waved the butterfly net with the other as he set off through the garden, past the pit where no one had found any treasure, and along the zig-zag path that led up Griffon Hill. Up and up he went, huffing and puffing like a little tartan steam engine, this way and that, swooping and scooping with the butterfly net, almost but never quite catching his sad, flyaway story. The path ended, but Mr. Ingoldsby could hear the vast soft voice of the late summer night whispering, 'I weep for the death of the griffons, those noble beasts of the world's morning.' Path or no path he went on, leaping and scooping but never quite catching his runaway pages though his story was being whispered in the very air around him.

Suddenly something moved above him and the moon seemed to go behind a cloud. Mr. Ingoldsby had run between two great paws, like the paws of a lion but much bigger. He looked up and then up still further. What seemed just another one of the strangely shaped rocks of Griffon Hill was a huge creature, part eagle, part lion, sitting back on its hind legs, slowly folding its wings behind it and turning its head down to look at him. It had a hooked beak and wild dark eyes, each one reflecting a full moon so that it seemed to have pupils of silver fire. Mr. Ingoldsby was standing between the paws of a fabulous beast . . . perhaps the original and ancient griffon that had given Griffon Hill its name. Its front legs were the claws of an eagle and in its right claw it held the flighty page of Mr. Ingoldsby's story.

'So it's you that has been covering the hill with these tumbling pages,' it said. 'That's spreading litter, that is, and the punishment is a very tasty one.'

'Tasty?' quavered Mr. Ingoldsby, overwhelmed by the size and the power of the fabulous Griffon.

'Tasty for me, that is,' the Griffon said. 'You'll have to be eaten. If we griffons catch anyone throwing wastepaper around on our hill we're allowed to eat them. It's a very old law and a lot of people have forgotten about it but it's in the books.'

'I didn't know,' Mr. Ingoldsby said hastily.

'No excuse! Ignorance of the law is no excuse,' replied the griffon snapping its sharp beak—rather unpleasantly. 'You've been spreading wastepaper and must pay the penalty.'

'But it isn't really wastepaper,' Mr Ingoldsby cried. 'This is a story that I happened to lose earlier in the day. I was just trying to find it again. You could see that for yourself.'

The Griffon lifted its crest in sudden interest. 'A story?' it cried. 'A real old-fashioned sort of story? A tale? One I haven't heard before?'

'You won't have heard this one. It's just been written this afternoon,' said Mr. Ingoldsby boldly. 'It wasn't there this morning.'

'I haven't heard a story in years, not a new one, that is,' the Griffon said. 'Of course we've never ever given up telling the old ones. I do hope it's funny. I like a good laugh.'

Mr. Ingoldsby sighed. 'Not very funny,' he had to confess. 'It's rather sad.'

'I'm not so fond of sad stories,' said the Griffon looking thoughtful. 'I'll tell you what . . . you read it and I'll see what I think of it. If I think it's rubbish after all, I'll eat you, but if I happen to like it I'll let you go. Does that seem fair?'

'Not very,' Mr. Ingoldsby replied.

'Well, let's put it like this . . .' said the Griffon. 'It's almost too fair from a griffon's point of view. I know some griffons who would make you read the story and then eat you anyway, no matter whether it was good or bad. Many griffons would think I was being unnaturally soft-hearted.'

45

'I don't have the rest of the story,' Mr. Ingoldsby said, but the Griffon lifted its huge tail which was almost exactly like a lion's tail, except that it ended in a point rather like the tip of a spear, and there, spiked neatly through each right-hand corner, were all the pages of Mr. Ingoldsby's only sad story.

So there was nothing for it . . . he sat like a tartan gnome shuffling his pages and putting them into order while his companion looked over his shoulder with interested, moony eyes. Mr. Ingoldsby did think of making a run for it but the Griffon, almost as if it was reading his thoughts, put its right front claws through the hem of his dressing-gown. There was nothing for it but to begin reading . . . reading by the moonlight caught and reflected and magnified by the Griffon's great eyes.

'I weep for the death of the griffons, those noble beasts of the world's morning.' He nearly choked with terror but the Griffon merely sighed and seemed to settle down to listen even more closely, so he went on. At first he read hesitating and stammering with fear, but the story—his only sad story—was stronger than his fear. He began to forget that he was a little fat man with a bad temper and a tartan dressing-gown who might be eaten at any moment, and he became simply a voice that the story was using to tell itself. In the small space between the Griffon's paws he stamped up and down waving his hands, while tears at his own words poured down his cheeks, and read his only sad story like a man singing a new song. Above him the Griffon listened in silence, and beyond the Griffon, the hill and the shiny night listened too. At last he came to the final page and the story ended, as it had begun, with tears for the passing of the griffons, the noble beasts of the world's morning.

Then Mr. Ingoldsby grew quiet and the mysteriousness of Griffon Hill crept back around him. He remembered who he was and that he lost his temper too much, and that he had been telling a griffon story to a griffon on Griffon's Hill, prancing around like a piece of tumbling wastepaper himself.

'Go on, eat me,' he said, and wished he had taken his boys swimming every weekend, feeling sad for the time with them hat he had missed. He looked up bravely at the fierce eagle face above him. Beside the moon reflected in each of its eyes he saw a star that swelled and changed and became a silver comet running shimmering down to the cruel beak. The Griffon was crying too.

Two enormous tears fell with a silvery splash at Mr. Ingoldsby's feet and then rolled like great pearls down the hillside. Then two more tears fell and another two.

'How beautiful,' said the Griffon at last. 'How truly beautiful. How did you come to understand so much about griffons?'

'Perhaps it's living at the foot of Griffon Hill,' Mr. Ingoldsby suggested. 'Perhaps I've picked some griffonish feeling out of the air.'

'Have you any more stories like that?' asked the fabulous creature eagerly.

'Well no . . . it's been very difficult . . .' Mr. Ingoldsby began, and before he knew what he was doing he was explaining all about his funny stories, and the sad stories that nobody would be interested in.

'I'm interested,' said the Griffon. 'I didn't think I would be but I am. And not only that, other griffons will be too. We're not really dead, as you can see. We've crept down into the heart of the world and only come out at full moon, just to check up on things. And griffons enjoy a good cry though it takes a lot to get them going. Mere sadness isn't enough. Griffons need power and poetry and a feeling of passing time. Now read your story all over again and I'll just sit here and drink it in. And then we'll see if we can't come to some arrangement—as between a griffon and a near neighbour.'

Mr. Ingoldsby came staggering home in the early morning. The wind had died down and the sky was starting to be blue. The horizon, hung with flags of gold, was getting ready to welcome the sun, while over in the west the moon was going down. Everything in the world seemed beautiful and perfectly in balance, even Mr. Ingoldsby himself. He had read his story over and over again to the Griffon and though he did not read it

47

as well as he had read it the first time, the Griffon had wept its great pearly tears at every repetition. Mr. Ingoldsby had promised to write more sad stories and to come back to read them to the Griffon Hill griffons at the time of the next full moon. He felt very much at ease with the world as he came down the last slope to his back gate. Even the thought of frivolous fiction and merry memoirs did not worry him. In fact he found himself rather looking forward to writing them again. Someone was calling him. 'Dad! Dad!' He looked around, suddenly dazzled for the thin bright rind of the sun pushed itself up above the horizon at that moment and reflected straight into his eyes. But what was it reflecting from? Martin and Micky, very dashing and cheerful in towels and swimming togs, came shouting out of the daze and dazzle.

'How did you manage it? It's brilliant,' they cried.

It *was* brilliant too. The stone pit where nobody had ever found any treasure was filled with wonderful warm salty water clear as crystal but with moonlight and starlight caught in its depths. Mr. Ingoldsby saw at once what had happened. The Griffon's tears had rolled down the hill and had filled the pit turning it into a little warm lake deep enough for diving, just right for every kind of swimming. It was almost like having a midsummer seaside on your very doorstep. Martin and Micky knew their father had arranged it somehow but they couldn't work out just how, and their father didn't tell them. A man has to keep some secrets to himself.

And ever afterwards Mr. Ingoldsby was as chirpy as a cricket—writing funny stories during the week, just as he always had. But at the weekends he wrote stories of beautiful sadness and every full moon he climbed up Griffon Hill to read them not only to his own Griffon but to the Griffon's beautiful griffon wife and aged griffon parents who listened, enraptured, to the melodious and melancholy tales. Sometimes, quite frequently really, they wept great tears that topped up the old treasure-pit with water that was warm but still sparkling so that Martin and Micky swam every day and their friends often came to swim too. Martin and Micky quickly became swimming

48

hampions at their school, darting through the water like
moonbeams. For who could help being a very special swimmer
he practised in the tears of the fabulous griffons of Griffon
Hill?

The Pumpkins of Witch Crunch

There were once three old men who lived side by side in a sma
country town. Mr. Hawthorne lived on the right side, and M
Lavender lived on the left side. But Mr. Maverick-Mace live
between them. 'A rose between two thorns,' he used to say
though everyone else thought it was a thorn between two rose
for Mr. Maverick-Mace was a very prickly man.

These three were very keen gardeners. They all gre
flowers and vegetables, but their gardens were quite differer
from one another. Mr. Hawthorne's garden sprawled an
tumbled and mingled. The cabbages wandered in among th
daffodils and columbines nodded to each other across th
carrots. Mr. Maverick-Mace looked over his fence and sniffe
scornfully. Mr. Lavender's garden was much neater, but
great tree grew on the lawn and spread its roots as if the tree wa
laying a trap for him.

'You should cut that tree down,' Mr. Maverick-Mace tol
him. 'You'll never have a garden until you do. Besides, th
roots spread under my garden too.'

'Oh well, the birds love it,' said Mr. Lavender, 'and so d
I.' He rolled his lawn smooth and made a bird-bath in the gree
shade of the tree. Around its knobby roots he planted crocuses
and put a little ladder up into its big broad branches so tha
children could climb it if they came to call.

Mr. Maverick-Mace's garden was more like an army drill
ing than a garden growing. The plants went in straight line
and the ground around them was bare and brown like a parad
ground. Mostly Mr. Maverick-Mace grew vegetables which h
sold, but he had a few flowers too which he entered for flowe
shows. They were bigger and brighter than any flowers which
Mr. Hawthorne or Mr. Lavender grew. But he always had to b
busy protecting them from wind and rain and cold. He either
crowded them into a tiny glasshouse which he had at the back

f his house or tied plastic bags over them. If he saw anyone
ooking over his hedge, staring at these odd flowers in their
plastic bags, Mr. Maverick-Mace felt sure they were planning
o steal them. He frowned and became very rude until whoever
t was hurried on.

'Why be like that?' said Mr. Hawthorne to him. 'No one
round here is a thief. No one touches my garden or Mr.
Lavender's except the children who come to visit us.'

'That's all very well, Hawthorne,' said Mr. Maverick-
Mace, 'but my garden is full of prize plants, whereas yours
s half jumble and half weeds. You just can't compare
our garden with mine,' and puffing up with conceit, Mr.
Maverick-Mace walked off to shout soldierly orders to his
errified and cowering silver beet.

Now, up the road from the three gardeners was a small
piece of land left over when houses were built in that part of
own. On this triangle of grass and broom bushes sat a brown
caravan, looking as if it had grown there—as if it had long,
ecret roots going down into the ground. In it lived a little
woman, as brown and battered as the caravan. She wore red-
and-white striped stockings, and skirts bright with patches and
uneven around the hem. 'My skirts and petticoats are *my*
garden,' she would tell Mr. Lavender and Mr. Hawthorne.
'Every time I sew a patch on it's like planting a new flower.'

Her caravan had a sunny doorway, and over it hung a cage
with a canary in it, and in this doorway she would sit in the
evenings playing on her battered accordion while the canary
sang a song to keep her company. Needless to say, Mr.
Maverick-Mace did not speak to this old woman. He suspected
he might be after his prize flowers or be wishing to break the
neat ranks of his carrots. When she came down the road to the
shop he watched her narrowly from behind his curtains. Once
he had actually seen her rest her hand on his gate as she talked
to Mr. Hawthorne.

'Just let me catch her,' muttered Mr. Maverick-Mace. 'She
wouldn't forget what *I'd* have to say to her!'

The old woman's name was Mrs. Mehetibel.

51

One spring the word got about that pumpkins were going to b
short that season, and Mr. Maverick-Mace immediately set ou
to plant some. He did not usually plant pumpkins for h
disliked their straggly gipsy ways and despised them for pee
ing over fences as if to see what was going on. Mr. Maveric
Mace did not care for such behaviour. However, he thought
was worth putting up with pumpkins if they were going to b
scarce. He reckoned he might make his fortune.

As he was bent over his garden a voice came across the fro
fence. To his horror he saw it was Mrs Mehetibel.

'Good morning . . .' she called out.

'Morning,' he said in a gruff, unfriendly fashion.

'You've got a fine garden there,' the voice went on.

'Why's she so friendly all of a sudden?' Mr. Maverick-Ma
wondered and did not bother to answer.

'And your cabbages are lovely,' the voice said plaintive
'I'm very partial to a taste of cabbage. You couldn't spare on
from the end of the row for a poor old woman, could you?

Mr. Maverick-Mace stood up furiously. 'No, Madam,
couldn't,' he declared. 'It would spoil the appearance of t
row for one thing, and for another I don't grow cabbages to gi
away. I grow them to sell for money, not for any old witch
beg for—after I've done all the work, too.'

There was silence for a moment, then the voice replie
'Witch you have said, witch it shall be.' And shuffling feet we
on up the road. Mr. Maverick-Mace blinked after her, sud
denly feeling alarmed. 'That *was* Mrs. Mehetibel, wasn
it? . . . That patched figure with the red scarf tied around h
head. The voice was certainly hers—or was it?' wondered M
Maverick-Mace. 'Wasn't it just a little different?'

Up popped Mr. Lavender, looking over the left-han
hedge. 'You're a brave man,' he said.

'He's a silly one,' cried Mr. Hawthorne, nodding over th
right-hand fence.

'To speak to Mrs. Mehetibel's sister like that!' marvelle
Mr. Lavender.

'Her sister?' Mr. Maverick-Mace repeated.

'Her twin sister—the well-known witch, Ginger Crunch,' Mr. Hawthorne declared. 'I try to be polite to everyone, but I'd be *extra* polite to Ginger Crunch.'

'I don't believe in witches,' said Mr. Maverick-Mace in a very sulky voice. 'Leave me to get on with my gardening.'

But when he came to plant the pumpkin seeds, he found they had turned blue. This made him thoughtful for a moment. Then he laughed. . . . 'Why, if the pumpkins grow blue it will make my fortune all the same. People may not want to eat them, but they'll pay to look at them. Scientists and museums from all over the world will want to buy them.'

He could hardly wait for the pumpkins to start growing, but when they did, they were just ordinary pumpkins, apart from coming up a week earlier than he had expected. Mr. Maverick-Mace was quite disappointed. He was so sharp and scolding with the rest of his garden that two rows of red radishes turned into white ones.

At first the pumpkins grew away quietly by themselves. They were fine and green and Mr. Maverick-Mace grinned with delight, thinking of the hundreds of pumpkins he would be able to sell. He heard on the radio that other people's pumpkins were limp and dejected that year and it pleased him enormously. 'I can just hear the money clinking and rustling in,' he muttered.

The pumpkins grew and grew. They put out green arms and a thousand twining fingers. They went up over Mr. Hawthorne's fence and terrified his sweet peas. They crawled out towards Mr. Maverick-Mace's onion beds like leafy cater-pillars. Now Mr. Maverick-Mace was not quite so happy. The onions grew nervous and shuffled out of line, spoiling the look of the garden. 'You pumpkins!' grumbled Mr. Maverick-Mace. 'Never mind!' He cheered up a bit. 'It's good to see you growing so well. I've never seen pumpkins grow like that!'

A rustle ran through the pumpkins as if a breeze was stirring their leaves.

'Bless them, they're so clever. You'd think they were trying to reply,' Mr. Maverick-Mace remarked fondly.

'They're a good deal *too* clever for me,' Mr. Hawthorne said over the fence. 'I don't like the way they're spreading out so quickly. It isn't natural for plants to grow so much. You can practically *see* them move over the ground.'

'Jealousy!' thought Mr. Maverick-Mace. Aloud he said, 'Oh well, I put them in with 'Swish'—the wonder pumpkin food. It must be doing them good.'

'It's doing them too much good,' said Mr. Hawthorne. He slapped away a wandering tendril of pumpkin that seemed to be trying to snatch off his glasses. 'Those aren't pumpkins—those are pets, and not very well-trained ones. You need to have them on a collar and chain and to get a licence to keep them. In a little while you'll be able to take them out for walks.'

'Jealous!' thought Mr. Maverick-Mace again. It was good to think that other people were envious of his pumpkins.

But the next morning he was not at all pleased. He woke to find that the pumpkins had spread themselves like a green carpet over the onions and were busy pulling out the carrots. Mr. Maverick-Mace was furious. 'I'll show you, you pestilential pumpkins,' he shouted. 'I'll rip you! I'll clip you!' He ran for the garden shears. As he returned with the shears a curious thing happened. The pumpkins started to rustle and hiss. Their great leaves stirred as if a wind was blowing over them and then began to toss like an angry sea. Their arms stretched out among the carrots and reared up like angry blind serpents.

Suddenly Mr. Maverick-Mace was terrified. 'There's no need to be like that about it,' he said plaintively. 'I really wouldn't dream of snipping you or clipping you. I just want to prune the hedge a little.' He sidled away from the pumpkins. As he attacked the innocent hedge, he could feel the pumpkins watching him and whispering to each other about him. Mr. Maverick-Mace did not quite dare to turn his back on the pumpkins, but he did not want to watch them either. At last he scuttled inside and read his Savings Bank Deposit Book to calm himself.

The next few days were the most uncomfortable Mr. Maverick-Mace had ever spent. His garden was not his own

ny more. It belonged to the fiendish green pumpkins. They
ulled out his carrots, and played marbles with his radishes,
nd surged on like a wild sea to the lettuces. Then the beetroots
anished and there seemed to be nothing Mr. Maverick-Mace
ould do about it. Every now and then he would go rushing out
ith the scissors or an axe—or anything—to cut back the
ebellious pumpkin plants. But the pumpkins always knew he
as there and hissed at him furiously, lifting up their snaky
rms to threaten him. Mr. Maverick-Mace was too scared to
hreaten them back.

Then one night as he sat trying to read his old gardening
agazines something happened—something he had been wait-
g for: a shy tapping at his windows, the gentle scratching of a
housand green fingers.

'Go away,' whispered Mr. Maverick-Mace. 'Go away.' But
he pumpkins would not go away. They knocked more and
ore loudly. Then with a crash that sounded to poor cowering
Mr. Maverick-Mace like the world exploding, the door burst
pen, the windows broke and the pumpkins rushed in at him.

'Help! Help!' he yelled as loudly as he could. 'Help! Help!
he pumpkins are after me—Help! Help!'

In the cottage on the right Mr. Hawthorne woke. In the
ouse on the left Mr. Lavender put down his paper. Then
ogether they rushed out to grapple with the terrible pumpkins
nd to rescue Mr. Maverick-Mace. Mr. Hawthorne carried an

old sword his great-grandfather had worn into battle. M[r]
Lavender arrived seated on his great green motor-mower an[d]
both of them attacked the pumpkins which now were wavi[ng]
and surging and hissing like an angry sea. At first they took th[e]
pumpkins by surprise. The motor-mower slashed into the[m]
and Mr. Hawthorne's waving sword whipped off several lon[g]
snaky arms. But the pumpkins soon realised what was happe[n]-
ing. They pushed their bristly leaves into the motor-mower an[d]
choked it. They dragged Mr. Lavender off and wrapped them[-]
selves around him. Mr. Hawthorne's sword was twitched fro[m]
his hand and a strong pumpkin arm twisted itself around h[is]
ankles and tripped him. They fought on furiously under th[e]
cool light of the moon, though it was obvious the pumpki[ns]
were winning easily. In fact, Mr. Lavender and Mr. Ha[w]-
thorne had almost given up trying to rescue Mr. Maveric[k]
Mace when they looked up and saw the sharp face of the witc[h]
Ginger Crunch watching them with some amusement.

'It's a fine night for a bit of excitement,' she observed, 'an[d]
the moonlight looks lovely on the pumpkins, doesn't it?'

Mr. Hawthorne and Mr. Lavender were too choked b[y]
pumpkins to reply.

'Ah well,' Ginger Crunch went on, 'I've no wish to har[m]
either of you gentlemen, so perhaps I'd better whistle my pe[t]

follow me. I'm off home now, back to my burrow in the hills.'

As she spoke, she took from her belt a long slender pipe and began to play a tune on it. The pumpkins stopped fighting and listened. It was plain to both Mr. Hawthorne and Mr. Lavender that the pumpkins were really listening. Then, leaving Mr. Lavender and Mr. Hawthorne lying on the ground bruised and breathless, that army of terrible pumpkins pulled up their own roots and like rippling serpents, gentle and docile, followed the witch Ginger Crunch and her strange piping tune. Down the hill she led them, and Mr. Hawthorne and Mr. Lavender, staggering to the gate, saw her, grey as a ghost in the moonlight, disappearing for ever around the corner with her strange pumpkins following, fawning and frolicking around her. As they stared, the door of the house burst open and Mr. Maverick-Mace stumbled out on to the verandah. His clothes were in rags and tags, his hair was standing on end and he had a black eye which he had given himself in the fury of his struggle with the pumpkins; but, bruises and all, he was alive and safe and so glad to see the last of the pumpkins that he wept like a baby and promised to lead a new life full of kindness and good deeds.

* * *

But alas, it takes more than being half choked by mad pump kins to change a man like Mr. Maverick-Mace. As soon as h black eye had gone he became as conceited and crotchety ever. It is doubtful if anything short of being run over by steam-roller could permanently improve Mr. Maverick-Mac However, there were two changes his friends noticed in hin One was that he stopped sneering at Mr. Lavender and his tre and remarking on Mr. Hawthorne's disorderly garden. Aft all, Mr. Lavender might have tree roots all the way under h lawn, and Mr. Hawthorne might be too easy-going with h flowers and vegetables, but at least they did not come tappin on the doors and breaking down the windows. The oth change in Mr. Maverick-Mace was that he was very careful be polite to Mrs. Mehetibel, to praise her canary, and to sen her bundles of vegetables in season. He was worried that sh might otherwise write to her twin sister, the fiendish Ging Crunch, and that one moonlight night those pumpkins mig come writhing and wriggling back up the hill to finish the work.

58

The World's Highest Tray Cloth

Last day of school,' said Helen in a pleased voice. 'We'll be out early.'

'Don't forget to come to the Shaws after school. I'm visiting Peggy Shaw this afternoon,' her mother told her. 'Come back with Rona.'

'Do I have to?' asked Helen in a whiny voice. 'I don't like Rona, and also she's finished her tea-tray cloth.'

'For goodness sake!' her mother replied sharply. 'I'd forgotten about that. It was meant to be finished by the end of term. Be sure to take it to school with you.'

'Do I have to?' asked Helen again. 'I'll get more marks if Mrs. Sinclair doesn't see it.'

But her mother got the tea-tray cloth from the sewing drawer and took it out of its plastic bag. 'It does look a bit chronic, doesn't it?' she said. 'Six weeks to do two rows of cross-stitch!'

'I've had to do them lots of times, though,' Helen explained. 'The crosses went all funny. You're supposed to count the threads but I just guess every now and then. I had to undo it, and do it over again and I got behind.'

'I'll say you did,' her mother said rather sarcastically. Then she added, 'You could have caught up by doing some at home, of course, instead of spending every spare minute of your time up those old trees.'

'But home-time's playing-time,' Helen cried. 'You don't want me to get sick with too much work, do you? Especially with that sewing!'

'Fat chance!' said her mother, grinning a bit.

'I'm no good at sewing,' said Helen seriously, 'and I am good at trees. I should stick to what I'm good at. I can get from one end of the line of trees to the other without having to come down to the ground once. And there's one branch that's hard to get to—you have to hang upside-down and then hook your arm and leg right over it and wriggle. . . .'

'That's all very well!' her mother said. 'Sewing will be useful to you someday and tree-climbing won't. Suppose you want to make a pretty dress one day . . .'

'Yuck!' said Helen.

'. . . or some blue jeans, then,' her mother went on. 'Climbing trees won't help you much.'

'If I was chased by a bull, it would be better to be good at climbing trees,' Helen argued. She could see the bull in her mind, red-eyed and furious, charging at her in vain as she leapt into a tree, and then hung upside-down, laughing, over the bull's angry horns.

'Oh Helen—for goodness sake,' her mother cried. 'You're not likely to be chased by a bull . . . Well, you're to hand your sewing in anyway,' she added, giving up argument and becoming bossy. 'And come back to the Shaws with Rona after school.'

Her mother went out of the room, but Helen stood by the window looking out into their garden. It was a square garden, bigger than most, with a concrete drive and a lawn and flowers. Two high hedges shut it in at the sides and it ended with a line of trees and a brown fence. Beyond the fence was a busy road, houses, shops and a whole town. Somewhere on the other side of the fence was a winding river, somewhere was the sea. But Helen could see none of these adventurous places even though she knew they were there. From the top branches of the tallest tree in the line she could see across many roofs to the school, she could look down into a builder's yard and watch trucks unloading timber and catch a glimpse of the river, but even the tallest tree in their yard could not make her as tall as she wanted to be.

Now, standing at the window, she looked sideways and could see a small spear of green almost like part of the hedge. But it was really the peak of the enormous pine tree standing by Ransome's dairy. No one could climb Ransome's pine tree for there were no branches close to the ground. Still, Helen liked to

60

look at it. You could see it from school and you could see it from the Shaws, which was a waste because nobody there was interested in trees. If you climbed to the top of Ransome's tree you would be able to see everywhere all at once, as if you had become a sort of magician with the whole world for your magic crystal.

At school that day it was just as Helen had thought it would be—all right until Mrs. Sinclair's handicraft class. There are lots of different sorts of handicrafts, but Mrs. Sinclair had been a a sewing teacher for years and she felt safest with sewing. Everyone had to sew something. Mrs. Sinclair was very keen on tray cloths. She must have been to blame for hundreds and hundreds of tray cloths, done in cross-stitch, running stitch, open buttonhole stitch and even herring-bone stitch. Rona Shaw's tray cloth came crisply out of its plastic bag, with the stitches even and the cream linen still clean. She had done some herring-bone stitches, and Helen, who liked the name herring-bone stitch, thought it might have been easier to do a stitch with an interesting name. Cross-stitch had started to sound dull and grumbling even before she had threaded her needle.

'Helen Hay!' Mrs. Sinclair cried. 'This is terrible! You haven't got it right yet. Look—it goes crooked here at the very end. You just haven't been counting your threads. And how did you get it so grubby! You can't have been keeping it in its plastic bag.'

'I kept it in the bag all the time,' said Helen indignantly, and it was true. She did not mention, however, that she had kept several other things in the plastic bag with the sewing, including two good smooth stones, a long piece of hairy string, two safety pins and a stub of brown chalk. The chalk, which was to blame for many of the marks on Helen's tray cloth was gone now, though the hairy string and the pins and one of the stones were safely stored in the pocket of her windcheater.

'I can't even give you a "C" for that,' declared Mrs. Sinclair, and she marked down C— in her book, changed her mind, crossed it out and wrote down D instead. Helen was glad that that was over, but she made up her mind not to walk home with

61

Rona. She could easily dodge her after school and if she turned up at the Shaws just a little late, she might miss out on any tray cloth conversation. Thinking of a way to escape she put her sewing back into its plastic bag, folded it in four, and scrunched it into the pocket of her windcheater.

In order to miss Rona, Helen got off to a good running start down a different street from the usual one. That was how she found herself going towards Ransome's house. The big pine tree swelled up like an island rising out of a sea of roofs. It was wide as well as tall, unusual in a pine tree, and spread out big branches on either side. At the ends of the branches cones huddled like families of perching birds and its deeply wrinkled bark, grey on the surface with reddish-brown showing through from below, gave it a grandfatherly look. It was planted on the right side of Ransome's house, not to interfere with sunshine, or telephone lines, though its roots had crept along under the ground and were crinkling the asphalt of the footpath. Helen thought it was a tree of power.

As she wandered by, staring at it, she suddenly saw something that interested her. Barry Ransome, his little brother Cedric and another boy, Peter Becket from down the road, were leaning a ladder against the trunk of the tree. She stopped and stared.

'What are you doing?' she called.

'None of your business,' Barry replied, breathless from ladder-carrying. They were going to climb the tree.

'Can I come too?' Helen asked.

Barry scarcely looked at her. 'No!' he said. 'This is just for us.'

Helen did not argue because she had already made her own plans. She watched the boys climb up the ladder and on to the first branch of the tree. It looked big enough to dance on.

They stood there for a moment—no hands—showing off a bit—and then began to climb up on to the next branch. Barry had to help Cedric whose hands were too small to get a proper grip on the rough bark.

Helen scrambled up the bank on to Ransome's lawn while

62

the boys were busy climbing. She took her shoes off and wriggled her toes until they felt properly alive. Then she climbed up the ladder and on to the branch on the opposite side of the tree from the climbing boys. The tree felt as solid as a house. Helen looked at it curiously. At some time when the tree was small someone had cut the centre out of it. That was why it had spread out so widely. Helen began to climb.

The cracked and wrinkled bark on the trunk of the tree was difficult to get a grip on, but the branches were much smoother and not too hard on the knees. Every now and then beads of gum like jewels of gold stood out on the bark as if the tree was oozing honey. The pine-tree smell reminded Helen of holidays so that she smiled as she climbed. It was easy climbing, the branches coming one after the other like steps in a staircase and no nasty little scratchy twigs to get in the way. The little Ransome, Cedric, suddenly saw her and stopped.

'Look—' he said, 'that girl's coming up.' Peter and Barry stopped, too, and looked around the trunk at her.

'Go on. Get down. You're not allowed up here,' Barry hissed. He was trying to speak quietly and Helen had a sudden thought.

'Are you allowed to?' she asked, and the boys were silent.

'Get down,' said Barry again.

'I don't have to,' Helen replied. She knew he could not make her, and that he did not want the sound of an argument to be heard up in the tree. She looked down.

'We're up quite high already,' she said speaking quietly, 'and there's still a long way to go.'

'Come on!' said Peter. 'We'll be able to see a long, long way when we get to the top.'

'I don't think I'm going any further,' Cedric mumbled. 'I'm too little.'

'I told you you were too little,' Barry replied crossly. 'Can you get down again?'

'I'll wait here till you come back,' Cedric muttered. 'I can easily hang on. Don't be too long though,' he added anxiously.

Peter and Barry climbed up on one side of the tree and

Helen climbed up on the other. On Helen's side a dead branch stuck out a little way from the tree. It was quite dry, broken off long ago. The boys had a good growing branch on their side, but on Helen's side it was as if there was a step missing. She wondered if she dared to trust the dead branch, if it would take all her weight, and she kicked at it a few times to make sure. It seemed safe and she could reach the next branch up with her hands. Curling her fingers around the branch above she stepped on to the dead one. If it broke she would be swinging by her fingers fifty metres up in the air. However it did not break. She hauled herself up on to the next branch safely and rested a moment feeling her heart thudding as tree-climbers' hearts sometimes do when they have just got over a risky bit.

Now she was level with Barry and Peter. The higher they climbed the thinner the branches became and the more carefully they had to plan their climbing.

'Hurry up,' yelled Cedric down below.

'Shut up!' Barry replied in a sort of whispered shout.

They were nearly at the top now and suddenly the tree seemed to have changed. Where everything had been solid and steady and reliable it now seemed flimsy and unsure. Branches moved a little, bent or swayed when weight was put upon them. Barry, Peter and Helen were huddled together now, for the trunk between them had grown thin and young, without the thick crinkled bark that had covered it at the beginning of their climb.

'Are there any branches on your side?' Helen asked. 'Good branches, I mean.'

'Nothing we can get our feet on,' Barry said. 'This one's too high for feet to reach to, and there are no good toeholds in the trunk any more.'

'Same on this side,' Helen mumbled. 'There isn't anything easy left.'

'Let's go down,' said Peter who had been looking through the branches at the ground far below. 'We've gone high enough, and we can't get any higher.' He looked rather sick, his freckles standing out more clearly than usual. Helen and Barry looked down too. Barry swallowed and licked his lips anxiously. Helen could see Cedric's round face turned up to them, the first big branches further down, and below that again she caught a glimpse of the ladder looking like a play-centre ladder made especially small for little children to play with. It was a long way down and it seemed a pity to be so close to the top and not to get there.

'I'm going to hang upside-down,' she said. 'Then I might be able to pull myself up on top of this branch. That's how I do it at home.'

'Don't,' said Peter, his freckles standing out more than ever.

Barry was silent. He looked down and licked his lips again.

Helen faced towards the trunk and locked her fingers around the overhead branch. Then she walked her feet up the trunk and quickly swung her legs up and hooked them around the branch so that she dangled below it like a little sloth. The bough moved a little, slanting itself down slightly under her weight.

Just for a moment Helen let her head hang back and saw something she had not noticed before. At the end of the branch there was an open space in the needles of the tree and she could see the town. It was like looking down a sloping tunnel or through a telescope turned towards the earth and seeing a tiny picture perfectly clear but very far away. There was the round-about in the centre of town and, further over, the Baptist church with the poplar beside it (tall but useless for climbing) stabbing like a dagger into a watery blue sky. There was the school beside a green handkerchief of football field and tennis court and there was a piece of the river, doodling along as if someone had scribbled through the town with silver chalk. And there was Helen's own house, its trees only a short smudgy green line, and here *she* was, hanging upside-down in Ransome's pine tree looking out from the unexplored green country to a land she knew by heart.

The upside-downness went right inside her—the upside-downness of then and now, of here and there. That very morning she had been at home looking at the top branches of

Ransome's pine tree and talking about hanging upside-down. Now, in the afternoon here she was, hanging upside-down in Ransome's pine tree and seeing her home far down below.

Suddenly Helen felt very strange. She felt she was going to fall through the branches of Ransome's pine and break like an egg on the grass below. She screwed up her eyes as the world of trees and houses rushed away from her in a sort of wild black dream, as she was sucked into a shaking angry darkness. But she could still feel the pine bark under her locked fingers and under the crook of her knees and she clung there thinking fiercely about the feel of the bark beneath her skin. Then when she had that firmly fixed in her mind she began to think about the branch beneath the bark, and the tree beneath the branch, and the ground beneath the tree, and the town upon the ground, and slowly the world came back to her again, made out of her thoughts, built up piece by piece as she used to build cities out of blocks when she was very small.

Then she thought her way back into herself—hands and knees first, legs on knees and arms on hands, shoulders on arms and head between shoulders, all complete. Helen Hay, tree-climbing champion and, maybe, if she could get to the top, a sort of magician who would see everything at once and understand the world. She opened her eyes, looked up and saw that, once she was on top of this branch, she could easily get a little further and really reach the top of Ransome's pine.

Now was the time—the time to let go with one hand—one arm over, one leg over, wriggle around after them. She felt a button come off her dress but she was on top of the branch, first lying then sitting astride it, as if the tree was her wild green horse that she must ride across the world until it stood still, trembling. Now she must draw her feet up under her and stand up. The trunk was so thin she could grip it easily. And there, just above her, was a cluster of three branches sloping upwards making a sort of crow's nest on the mast of the tree. She scrambled into the branches and was safe for a moment, held by the tree which had first tried to throw her down and now wanted to look after her.

Helen found that her knees and hands were shaking. Her palms were sore and stained brown with pine gum. Her hair was wet around her forehead as if she had been out in a cold fog and her face was wet too. Tears rolled down her cheeks though she did not feel as if she was crying, just that her eyes were overflowing. She looked up and saw the last spire of the tree and then nothing but blue sky. She looked down. Peter and Barry were staring up at her, their faces round and still.

'Are you O.K.?' Barry asked. His voice sounded strange. It was as if he was asking her, 'Are you a ghost?'

'Of course I'm O.K.,' Helen answered and began to feel O.K. straightaway.

'Then why are you crying?' Peter asked. He sounded as if he did not believe her—did not believe *in* her—as if she might disappear.

'The wind was stinging my eyes when I was hanging upside-down,' Helen said.

The boys suddenly came alive again.

'Gee!' said Peter shaking his head. 'Gee!'

'You looked really funny,' Barry told her. 'Not funny to laugh at—funny as if you were going to fall.'

'I'm used to climbing like that,' boasted Helen. 'I do it all the time at home. It's the same thing whether you're high up in the air or close to the ground.'

She slowly stood up in her crow's nest to reach as high as she could reach. There were no more possible branches. She was as high as she could go. Now she could see the town on all sides and the river winding between the houses back to the hills, or out between the houses on to the sea. Helen could see in all directions at once. She had become like her dream of the morning, a wise magician who could use the world as his crystal ball, or the king of a green island floating over the roofs of cities.

Now there was nothing to do but to go down again, but Helen did not want to go down just yet. She wanted to leave a sign that she had been there.

'Carve your name,' Barry suggested, waiting patiently two branches below.

'No knife!' Helen said. 'Perhaps I could write it.' She unzipped her windcheater pocket and felt inside to see if she could find a piece of pencil. But there was no pencil, only the tray cloth in its plastic bag.

A little later she climbed down, sliding over the branches while Peter and Barry told her where to put her feet. The rest was easy. They reached Cedric who looked at her in alarm.

'I thought you might fall down and knock me down too,' he told her reproachfully.

'No way!' said Helen confidently and was first down the ladder and on to the ground again.

They stood there staring up into the tree. It was not quite the same tree that it had been. It had changed because now they knew some of its ways and could remember them. Now they had power over the tree.

'There's that part with the toehold in the bark,' Barry said to Peter.

'You can just see that dead branch from here,' Helen said to anyone who was listening but mostly to herself.

Mrs. Ransome came out on to the verandah.

'What are you boys doing?' she shouted. 'Who put that ladder up there?' She hurried over the lawn, her high heels sinking into the grass. 'Don't you dare try climbing that tree,' she cried. 'Don't you dare. I'll call your father if I see you take one step up that ladder.' Then she smiled at Helen.

'I sometimes wish I had girls,' she said. 'Boys are such a worry, the things they think up.'

The children looked at each other but there was nothing they could say.

'I've got to go. I'm late,' Helen said, picking up her case and her socks and shoes.

'Won't your feet get cold, Helen?' said Mrs. Ransome, staring curiously at her bare feet.

'No—it's good for feet to get fresh air,' Helen replied.

'See you some time then,' Barry called after her as she went away. He sounded friendly and made her feel friendly back.

Helen was late arriving at the Shaws—three-quarters of an hour late, which did not seem much to a person who had stepped out of time altogether, who had been a magician stopping clocks with a frown. But it seemed a long time to her mother.

Rona's tray cloth lay on the table being admired by the Shaws' visitors.

'Where's *your* tray cloth, Helen?' asked Mrs. Shaw in a kind voice, offering cake.

'Gone,' Helen said, feeling hungry for cake and taking a big piece. 'Mine wasn't any use as a tray cloth so I used it for something else.'

'What else could you use it for?' asked Mrs. Shaw, sounding amused. 'There's nothing much else you could use a tray cloth for, is there?' But Helen's mother snapped, 'Helen—look at your hands, they're filthy.'

'That's not dirt—it's pine gum,' Helen said politely and her mother sighed, a cross sigh.

'Kids!' she said to Mrs. Shaw, and Mrs. Shaw and two other visiting women said, almost together, 'I know,' and sighed and shook their heads too.

'Holidays!' exclaimed Helen going home. 'These are going to be good holidays. I've had a sign that they are going to be good.'

'No more school lunches for a fortnight,' agreed her mother taking her hand. 'A change is as good as a rest.'

Helen walked on in silence. In a moment she would say to her mother, 'See Ransome's pine tree? See that white flag at the very top? That's my tray cloth tied there with hairy string and pinned with two safety-pins stuck through it into the tree-trunk. That's *my* tea-tray cloth with my crooked cross-stitch on it blowing in the wind at the top of Ransome's pine tree, watching the town and the river and the sea, doing a *real* thing and not just sitting on a lady's tea-tray getting tea spilt on it.' What would her mother say?

70

'How could you do anything so silly—so dangerous!'
. . . or . . . 'I didn't buy you that piece of linen to make a flag
for Ransome's pine tree.'

Perhaps she wouldn't tell her mother yet, because it was
sometimes hard to explain what you could see so clearly in your
own mind—that a flag was a better thing than a tray cloth any
day—and also because she wanted to have a little time to herself
with the memory of hanging upside-down, of losing the world
and of making it all come together again.

All through the holidays, when the wind blew in from the
sea Helen's flag—the highest tray cloth in the world—
flickered, reflecting the sun like a little light at the top of
Ransome's pine. Then one stormy night it blew away. But it
did not matter because by then Helen had worked out that the
world was full of tall trees and that she was the one who was
going to hang flags on top of them all.

The Boy Who Made Things Up

There was once a father who had a little boy. However, it was a bit of a waste for this father to have a boy, really, because he was much too interested in work. He worked all the week and then, at the weekends, he spent all his time under the car fixing it so that he would be able to go to work again the next week. You will understand he did not have much time to spend with his little boy. In fact, all the little boy ever saw of his father was a pair of boots sticking out from under the car. This was not much fun. With no father to tell him exciting stories, the boy had to make up his own stories. He became very good at making things up.

Well, one day the father's car broke down a long way from home and had to be taken away to a garage, and there was not much for the father to do at the weekend. He felt bare and unprotected with no car to crawl under. The space of hills and sky made him feel nervous. However, he decided to make the best of it all, and take his boy for a walk instead.

'Come on, Michael,' he called. 'We'll wander down to the cross-roads, shall we?' Michael was delighted to go for a walk with his father. He marched cheerfully along beside him, looking at him curiously. He wasn't used to seeing all of his father at the same time. After a while he said, 'Shall we just walk along, Dad, or shall we make some of it up?'

'Make some of it up?' said the puzzled father. 'Make what up? . . . Oh well, whatever *you* like, Michael,' he added in a kind voice.

'Shall we go by *that* path then?' said the little boy, pointing. Over the field ran a path that the father did not recognize. It was narrow, and a bit tangled, with foxgloves leaning over it, and bright stones poking through the ground.

'That's funny!' said the father. 'I've never seen that path before. There's no doubt you miss a lot by driving everywhere. Where does this path go?'

'It goes to the sea,' said Michael, leading the way, brushing the dew off the foxgloves.

'But the sea is fifty kilometres away,' cried the father. 'It can't lead to the sea.'

'We're making it up, remember,' said Michael.

'Oh, just pretending,' the father replied, as if everything was understood and ordinary again.

'The sea is on the other side of that little hill,' Michael went on, and the father was amazed to see the path hump itself into a little hill in front of them. At the same time a soft murmuring filled the air, as if giants were breathing quietly in their sleep. The father and Michael hurried up the little hill. There on the other side was the sea. The sand stretched a long way, starred with shells, striped with seaweed. There was no one else on all that long sunny shore. There weren't even any seagulls—just the sand, with the sea dancing along its edge.

'I told you. I told you,' yelled Michael, and charged on to the beach. His father followed him, frowning with amazement.

'If I'd known we were coming here,' he said, trying hard to make his voice sound ordinary, 'I'd have brought buckets and spades.'

'There are buckets and spades over by that log,' Michael told him. 'And our togs! Mine are wrapped up in a blue towel. What about yours?'

'Er . . .' said his father.

'Just make it up,' Michael cried. 'I'll make it up for you. An orange towel, almost new.'

The log lay, half in, half out of the sand, as if it was trying to burrow down and get away from the sun. There were the buckets and spades. There were the togs and towels.

'Swim first!' decided Michael. 'It's a bit coldish. Let's make it a warm day.'

Immediately the wind died down and the sunshine grew hotter. The father stood frowning at his orange towel, almost new.

'I'm ready,' Michael said, dancing before him. 'You're slow, Dad. Last one in is nothing but a sand-flea.' He sped,

73

running and jumping, into the waves. The sand-flea father followed.

'Be careful!' he shouted. 'Remember you can't swim, and I haven't done much swimming myself for a few years.'

'Say you're a wonderful swimmer!' suggested Michael. 'Say we can both swim to the islands.'

'The islands?' said the father. Sure enough, out on the horizon were islands scattered like seeds in the furrows of the sea.

The boy and his father swam out to the islands without getting in the least bit tired. The water was warm, yet tingling and as clear as green glass. Shoals of bright fish, as small and shiny as needles, followed them and tickled their feet. Down down, far down under the water, the sand shone silver with black fish all over it, like a night sky pulled inside out. The boy and his father swam in and out among the islands. Waves burst on the rocks around them and rainbows in the spray curled over their heads. Sometimes they swam on their fronts, peering down through the clear water, watching fish and sand.

'I could swim all day,' the father cried.

'But we've got to get back to our ice-creams,' declared Michael.

So they swam lazily back to the long, empty beach, still quiet except for the sighing, breathing sea.

'Here! Where will we get any ice-creams?' asked the father, frowning again. 'There are no shops.'

'Can't you understand how things work yet?' Michael cried despairingly. 'We make something up! Look!'

Far down the beach something was moving closer and closer. It was a tall thin man dressed in black and white squares, like a harlequin or a chess board. He was holding a blue frilly sunshade over his head with one hand and carrying a basket in the other. With his feet he furiously peddled a yellow bicycle. As he passed them he put the basket into Michael's hands. Then he turned his bicycle and rode straight into the sea. For a few minutes his blue sunshade bobbed above the water and then a green wave curled slowly over it, like a curtain.

74

coming down at a theatre. They couldn't see him any more

'See what I mean?' asked Michael. 'Much better than shop.'

The basket was full of ice-cream with nuts in it, and straw berries on top. The father looked very grown-up and though ful. After they had eaten the ice-cream, they played with the buckets and spades for a while, and then they decided it wa time to go back down the foxglove path. All the way home th father looked more and more thoughtful and grown-up Everytime he looked at Michael he blinked.

As soon as they got home, Michael was sent to wash hi hands—a thing that usually happens to boys. The father stoo beside the mother, drying up the dishes she was washing.

'Tell me, my dear,' he said, in a quiet, nervous voice. 'Doe Michael often make things up?'

'Oh yes!' said his mother. 'He's rather a lonely little boy an he's always making up some adventure. He's very good at it.'

'But,' said the father in a very astonished voice, 'he took m to the BEACH. We went SWIMMING. I got SUNBURNED. My shoe are full of SAND. And yet I *know* the sea is fifty kilometres away

'Oh yes,' said the mother very casually, 'I told you. He' very good at making things up. I've told you before, but yo were too busy listening to the car.'

'It's very strange—very strange,' said the father.

'But lots of fun!' the mother added.

'Yes, I suppose it is,' said the father. He thought som more.

'I don't think I'll spend so much time with the car from no on. Michael needs the guidance of a father. A father and so should see a lot of each other, don't you think?' he asked.

'Oh yes, I'm sure they should,' said the mother, and sh smiled a smile that was almost a grin at the saucer she wa washing.

The Tatty Patchwork
Rubbish Dump Dancers

Mrs. Polly and her granddaughter Selina were very poor. They had nothing to eat but porridge with a little milk and no sugar, and they were two months behind with the rent.

'No go!' said their landlord. 'Or rather, the other way round. You'll HAVE to go. And as you owe me so much money, well, I'll have to keep your furniture. I don't want to, mind, but I've got to pay the rates and mend the roof as well. Being a landlord isn't easy.'

'Alack the day!' wept Mrs. Polly. 'We have only the clothes we stand up in.'

'Never say die, Granny, never say die.' Selina patted her Granny's arm. 'I know just the place we can go to. There's a cave by the town dump with wild apple trees growing around it, and we can live there, rent free, like furry bears.'

'That it should come to this!' Mrs. Polly wept again, but Selina sang and danced right there on the street corner—'Dump diddle dump diddle dump, dump, dump!'—until Mrs. Polly stopped weeping and merely sighed, and then stopped sighing and started to smile, and then stopped smiling and started to laugh.

'Off we go then!' she said. 'Dump diddle dump—here we come,' and dump diddle dump—diddle dump dump dump they went, all the way to the cave which was velvet with moss and shaggy with ferns, very pleasant and green on a hot summer afternoon.

'What shall we do now, Selina?' asked Mrs. Polly.

'Gather and glean, Granny, gather and glean,' answered Selina. 'There's a whole dump full of leavings to choose from.'

So they went gathering and gleaning with a tribe of thin striped cats who lived at the dump and found everything that was needed to set up a comfortable home in the cave. Selina

gathered an old carpet and two chairs, lopsided but still si
upon-able and Mrs. Polly gleaned a washing tub that didn
leak very much if you didn't fill it too full. Then Selina gathere
a fine mattress slightly burnt by an electric blanket striking o
on its own, and Mrs. Polly gleaned a big soft sofa, gone a
floppy like a St. Bernard dog, with broken springs. While the
gathered and gleaned, up roared the dump trucks filled wit
sweepings and scourings, weeds and white elephants, whic
they emptied out in a lonely corner of the dump. There wer
things that nobody wanted like old tea-leaves and coff
grounds, sad broken toys and poor torn books. But there wer
also a lot of scrips and scraps, a lot of whim-wham wigmaleer
stuff that could be useful if you didn't mind a few scratches an
patches.

'What shall we do now, Selina?' asked Mrs. Polly, thoug
she was beginning to catch on.

'Scavenge and save, Granny, scavenge and save,' replie
Selina.

Now in her scavenging Mrs. Polly found a big bag full
off-cuts from a dress factory, all the sweepings from the factor
floor, bits of silk, squares of satin and velvet. And curiousl
enough, next to all this useful stuff, was a rusty, dusty sewin
machine covered with eggshells but looking as if it might b
able to be made to work if one wanted to make it work har
enough.

> 'Little Stitcher, Little Stitcher
> Do you sew, do you sew?'

asked Mrs. Polly, for there was something about the o
machine that made her very polite to it.

And the machine actually turned its wheel a little bit an
answered in a rusty voice,

> 'Crazy stitches, crazy stitches!'

In her scavenging Selina found an old piano hidden under
heap of hedge-clippings, smiling up with a hopeful, yellov
smile.

'Old Smiler, Old Smiler
Do you play? Do you play?'

whispered Selina, for there was something about the old machine that made her respect it. And the old piano actually twangled a few wild notes and answered,

'Crazy music! Crazy music.'

One way and another Mrs. Polly and Selina got Little Stitcher the sewing machine and Old Smiler the piano into their green cave. Mrs. Polly stitched and sewed on Little Stitcher who went in a very hit and miss, cut and thrust fashion.

'Crazy stitches, crazy stitches!' murmured Mrs. Polly but she smiled as she said it, and made two tatty patchwork petticoats and two tatty patchwork hats, two tatty patchwork dresses and two tatty patchwork jackets.

Dressed in these Mrs. Polly and Selina were like wildflowers growing on the edge of the dump and now, of course, they wanted to dance and make merry. So Mrs. Polly sat down at Old Smiler and began to play, and—what a surprise!— Old Smiler played tatty patchwork music, for some keys refused to play at all and other keys made up for it by playing two notes at once. Mrs. Polly twangled away and Selina danced, her plum-purple-pink-patched skirts swirling around her ankles.

'Great green whiskers!' exclaimed Mrs. Polly. 'We've wound up with all that the heart could desire—song and dance both, a bit of colour to our clothes and a nice cave both cool and cosy. We've never had it so good.'

'We've got Little Stitcher and Old Smiler and a whole dump full of pets,' Selina said, watching the cats lick the thrown out fishbones until they were as white and beautiful as harps of ivory.

'Crazy music keeps us going and crazy stitches hold us together,' Mrs. Polly added contentedly.

And so they went on through the tatty patchwork summer.

When autumn came the wild apples on the apple trees

turned red and the wind got colder. The dump cats began to grow winter coats and Mrs. Polly and Selina began to feel winter's white dogs nipping at their heels with teeth of ice.

'We must dance harder, Granny,' Selina said. 'Hard dancing will keep us warm and well.'

They did not know, of course, that across the country in another town the King had been taken poorly.

'He is suffering from Autumnal Melancholy,' the royal doctors said. 'It goes around a lot at this time of year and even kings get it from time to time. He should go travelling, see new sights, the otherness of different places, the placiness of different others, and so on and so forth. He must go for a royal tour and we'll come too.'

The King set out at once in the royal car with a convoy of doctors following him on their medical motor-bikes. Wherever he stopped new clothes, exquisitely made, were brought to him, remarkable meals wonderfully cooked were served to him, classical music was played to him, note following note in grave and beautiful processions. The King stroked his clothes, tasted his food, listened to music and sighed. The doctors took his temperature, felt his pulse, looked deep into his eyes, and sighed too.

'The Autumnal Melancholy is getting worse,' they murmured.

'I'd like something a bit wilder to happen, I think,' said the King.

'All right,' the doctors told the Prime Minister. 'We'll have a Royal Barbecue for the King at the very next town we come to.'

The Royal Barbecue was held in a green park with high walls around it so that the common herd could not see the King's sausages getting turned over on the golden barbecue specially made for the King's cook.

The King, shimmering in a robe of silver silk, sat on a chair of gold, made soft with velvet cushions, and beside him stood the finest string quartet in the land playing tunes as playful and beautiful as trained white deer leaping through hoops of roses.

A sausage was brought to the King on a golden plate. He looked at it and pushed it away pettishly.

'Look at that!' muttered the doctors. 'Autumnal Melancholy at its very worst.'

But a breeze blew over the wall, and the King lifted his head, for the breeze brought music with it, like a tattered companion. Such music! It began, stopped, and started again, skipped two notes, went right for three, sounded the next note flat, went well for four and then sounded the next note sharp. It was a tune that danced on a peg leg, hopping and happy-go-lucky, almost, but never quite, falling over.

'That music!' said the King.

'We'll have it stopped,' said the Mayor of that town, his mouth full of royal sausage.

'No!' said the King. 'I like it. Where is it coming from?'

'Your Majesty,' said the Mayor, stammering rather, 'I can't be totally sure—I merely speculate—I'm not certain, you understand—but I think it's coming from the town dump.'

'The Municipal Refuse Disposal Precincts!' said a Councillor, trying to make it sound a bit more presentable.

'Ugh! Your Majesty, Ugh!' shouted the doctors. 'Don't listen to that music, Your Royalty! That music is crawling with germs. That music is smothered in old tea-leaves, last week's gravy, old macaroni that the dogs won't eat and millions of virulent microbes into the bargain. Don't let such infected melody into the royal ears. Don't listen to it.'

Everyone except the King covered their ears for fear of germs. But the King said, 'I like it. I like the way it dances and almost falls over. I'm off to find it.' And he bolted out of the park before his doctors could stop him.

'I won't be answerable for this,' yelled an Ear, Nose and Throat specialist.

'It needs looking into,' declared an optometrist.

The King came to the dump and stared at what he saw.

The music was coming from a green ferny cave in front of which danced a little girl with long red hair and a tatty patchwork skirt all plum-purple and patched with pink. With her

81

anced forty-seven striped cats while fully forty-seven others
joined in the music, playing on fishbone harps and old milk
bottles, making a sort of glassy rippling rhythm very pleasant
to hear.

The King watched in amazement and envy.

'Who is this child?' he cried. 'Who are these cats?'

'I don't know,' the Mayor admitted. 'I'll have them
arrested at once.'

But at the sound of his voice the cats scattered like spilt
striped brandyballs, and Selina stopped her dancing. The King
came towards her.

'No, your Majesty, no!' shouted the doctors as one doctor.
'Microbes and germs! Microbes and germs!'

The King took no notice. At the mouth of the cave an
elderly lady in plum-purple patched like a rainbow appeared
through the ferns.

'What's all this fuss?' she cried. 'Who has stopped the
dancing? Who has scared the cats?'

'I'm afraid it was me,' said the King, 'but play again and I'll
dance too.'

Mrs. Polly looked at him with scorn.

'It won't work with anyone wearing a crown, Your Majesty,
likewise it won't work for anyone in silk and satin. We tatty
patchwork dancers dance only in patchwork.'

But when she saw the expression of despair and desolation
on the royal face Mrs. Polly relented. 'I'll tell you what!' she
said. 'We're very much of a height, me being tall for a grand-
mother and you on the short side for a king. I'll lend you my
tatty patchwork trouser suit if you like.'

'Germs, germs, germs!' yelled the doctors who didn't like
to come too close for fear of infection. But the King hung his
crown on a wild apple tree and put on Mrs. Polly's trouser suit,
and then he danced with Selina while Mrs. Polly played Old
Smiler. He frisked and he whisked both high and low and
invented some dance steps that were to be fashionable for many
years to come. In between he and Selina ate the wild apples,
being careful to eat around the worm holes. At last Selina and

Mrs. Polly were both well and truly warm, and the King wa
well and truly cured of his Autumnal Melancholy.

'What a glorious evening!' he cried. 'I can see why you liv
in the dump. The music is so good and the dancing is wonder
ful.'

'Well, the music and dancing weren't here before we came,
Mrs. Polly said rather sternly, 'and my Selina and me—we onl
live here because nowhere else will have us. Likewise we've go
to dance to keep warm. It isn't just for the fun of it.'

'Fancy that!' said the King thoughtfully. 'Well, come bac
to the Royal Mansion and have a bite of supper with me.'

So that is what they did.

When the doctors got the King home they examined hin
from top to toe and were astonished to find that every sympton
had vanished. They were astounded, but all they could do wa
shrug their shoulders and disinfect the King who had becom
very rebellious.

'Dear Mrs. Polly,' he cried.

'Call me Polly,' said that lady who was, by now, on informa
terms with the King, 'for I'm Polly first as well as last.'

'Dear Polly,' the King said. 'Come back with me to m
castle in the Capital City and then you'll be on hand if th
dreaded symptoms strike again.'

'You'd better come,' the doctors told her. 'You've don
him a lot of good, so it's your patriotic duty. We'll have you an
Selina disinfected too.'

'I'll have to bring Little Stitcher and Old Smiler too,' Mrs
Polly cried, 'and all my tumbledown furnishings and garnish
ings, my gleanings and my gatherings. It wouldn't be like hom
to me without them.'

'All right, agreed!' the King nodded. 'Mind you, I draw th
line at all those cats.'

'They wouldn't come anyway,' Selina said. 'They prefer t
live in the dump diddle dump diddle dump dump dump.'

Mrs. Polly and Selina did so much good that he never go
Autumnal Melancholy again. Just to be on the safe side h
married Mrs. Polly, who became the Queen, and he adopte

84

Selina, who became a princess. Mrs. Polly made her own wedding dress and Selina's bridesmaid's gown and the King's wedding suit on Little Stitcher and it was the best Royal Wedding for five hundred years. After this, any subject with a problem would drop in at the castle for a cup of tea and good advice. After giving the good advice Mrs. Polly, Selina and the King would put on their tatty patchwork wedding clothes, all leaf-green, plum-purple, sunshine-yellow, petal-pink and sky-blue. Then they would play crazy hop-and-go-carry-one music to the sad visitor and dance with him until everyone's troubles went whirling away, like seagulls in a salt wind from the sea.

The Travelling Boy and
the Stay-at-Home Bird

Sam lived with his anxious Great Aunt Angela in a house with high hedges and a closed gate. When she was behind her high hedge with the gate slammed shut Great Aunt Angela was happy. Jaunts, junkets and journeys worried her to bits, but a closed gate soothed her, smoothed her, made her feel serene. In her little sun-porch she would knit and sew and sing like a spring blackbird and, sometimes, snatch a catnap as well, whereas a journey, even to the shops, made her go all fidgety and fretful. At such times she became a very difficult Great Aunt for a boy like Sam.

Sam had eyes halfway between sky-blue and sea-green. You never saw a boy with such a look of distance about him. There were a thousand journeys locked up inside him waiting to get out.

'Go here! Go there! Walk! Run! Skate! Sail! Fly!' said the voices in his head. 'Get there somehow!' But Sam was not allowed to do any of these things. The gate was always shut, and he was forbidden to go into the dirty, dangerous world outside.

Sometimes, however, Great Aunt Angela, though rather short-sighted herself, saw Sam's blue-green look of distance and overheard the echo of the voices inside his head.

'I suppose he needs some lively company,' she thought. 'I'm not very fond of animals, but perhaps a good, clean pet of some kind . . .' and, very bravely, she put on her boots and her good going-out coat, took her shopping trolley and called Sam. Then they set out together to visit the Paramount Pet Shop, which was all of two corners away. They crossed the street when the traffic-lights told them to cross and Sam could see four roads, all going in different directions. One road led to the sea, another to the mountains, one pointed to the South

Pole and another to the Equator. He was surrounded by possible journeys and all the roads seemed to be saying, 'Take me! Take me!'

Men had made a hole in the street and its black mouth hissed, 'Down here! Down here!' as Sam went by. He looked up and the sky was filled with travellers . . . a Piper Cherokee plane from the aero club, a couple of ducks in search of the river, and a whole crowd of sparrows, flying in every direction. 'Up and away! Up and away!' they cried, but only Sam could hear them.

Great Aunt Angela's own ears were too full of rattling footsteps, roaring cars, and raging trucks to hear the voices of possible journeys crying out to her.

When they got to the Paramount Pet Shop there were pets of all kinds to choose from—dogs, cats, guinea pigs, rabbits—but Great Aunt Angela did not want anything that would jump up, track in dirt on its paws, or have babies.

'What about a bird?' said the pet shop man, a very secret-looking man, unusual to find behind a public place like a shop counter. 'Their cages are very easy to clean. Sam could learn to do that for himself, couldn't you, Sam?'

'I don't want anything that has to live in a cage,' Sam said. 'I don't like cages.'

When the pet shop man heard this he gave Sam a very careful glance, and Sam stared back, and saw at once that the pet shop man was full of journeys too, but that his journeys had all been taken. He wore them openly on his face, which was lined like a map with the tracery of a thousand explorations.

'Why, I think I have just the pet for you, Sam,' he said at last. 'It's out the back because it's rather large.'

'I can't afford much!' cried Great Aunt Angela, anxious immediately. 'And we don't have much room.'

'Oh they're very cheap, these particular pets,' the pet shop man assured her. 'They're very hard to place because you've got to wait until the right customer comes along.' Then he went out into the back of the shop and returned a moment later with a bird following him . . . a tall bird, rather like a patchwork tea-cosy on long yellow legs, quite tame and looking as if it would be no trouble at all around the house.

'It's very brightly coloured,' Great Aunt Angela said nervously, for bright colours were part of the danger of the world to her.

'Oh, that could change,' the pet shop man said. 'He'll grow to whatever colour you need him to be. And he'll fit into any space you happen to have in the house. Fitting into available space is this bird's speciality. And he'll grow to the exact size that suits you.'

Great Aunt Angela was delighted to hear this. 'I do like him,' she decided. 'I love his blue eyes. We'll take him shall we, Sam, and we'll call him Norton after my late cousin Norton. He's got a look in his eyes that reminds me of dear Norton very strongly. You'll like that, won't you, Sam?'

'Yes thank you, Great Aunt Angela,' Sam replied.

But in his mind Sam called the bird Fernando Eagle, the freest name he could think of, a name for some buccaneer or bold adventurer who also happened to be a bird.

'He's too tame, really,' Sam thought. 'He's *over*tamed, but I'll un-tame him. I'll teach him to fight and fly and to be free, and when he does fly away at last—well, it will be almost as good as flying away myself. It will be a kind of promise to me that some day I'll be free too.'

Great Aunt Angela paid the money, and Sam and she walked home through the rattling, roaring, raging streets while Fernando Eagle stalked after them like a particularly well-behaved dog.

At home, with the gate closed and locked, Great Aunt Angela gave Sam and Fernando Eagle a slice of bread and jam each.

'He needs worms and wigglies, not bread and jam,' Sam cried.

'Oh Sam, don't say such things!' Great Aunt Angela exclaimed in alarm. 'I can't bear to think of worms and wigglies. And look—' she added triumphantly— 'he's eaten the bread and jam and he's asking for more.'

And so he had, and so he was.

'Good bird, Norton!' said Great Aunt Angela, patting him on the head.

Sam saw he had no time to lose and began his plans for the un-taming of Fernando Eagle immediately.

'He hasn't got a mother to teach him,' thought Sam, 'so I'll have to be a sort of mother to him.'

He tried to make himself as much like Fernando Eagle's mother as he could.

First he cut a bird mask out of cardboard but, when he tried it on, Fernando Eagle looked doubtful. Then he wrapped himself in an old curtain covered in red, white and blue squares, but Fernando Eagle merely sighed and shuffled his feet.

'Feet!' thought Sam and he cut himself big bird feet and stuck them on to the soles of his school shoes with sticky tape. Then he painted his new feet and his old legs (up above sock level) with yellow poster paint, and looked hopefully at Fernando Eagle. But Fernando Eagle sank his head deep into his ruff and clacked his beak in alarm.

'Now!' Sam cried. 'Listen! This is how eagles call,' and he hopped around the room giving wild dangerous cries of the sort he thought a free bird ought to give, as it took off into the sky. Such cries had never been heard behind the high hedge before. Out in the sun-porch Great Aunt Angela started as if she had been stung and dropped several stitches. Even so, she was not as frightened as Fernando Eagle who ran behind a chair and cowered there, terrified.

'Sam! Sam!' cried Great Aunt Angela as she burst into Sam's room. 'What a noise! Look at the room! Look at your legs! Look at those scraps of cardboard, look at your feet! Look at your face! Look at poor Norton, he's petrified, poor bird, and no wonder! Clean yourself up at once and then sweep the floor! Goodness gracious, what an example to set to an innocent pet barely in the house thirty minutes. He'll think you're some sort of hoodlum or noodlum, Sam.'

She went out of the room and Fernando Eagle scuttled after

her, anxious for quiet dignified company and more bread and jam. Sam was left to tidy up the mess he'd made. He was disappointed but not discouraged.

'It's a beginning,' he thought. 'I suppose it *is* pretty confusing for a bird before he realizes what he's supposed to do. But once he catches on he'll love it. Fancy being able to fly! I wish I could. I'll give him a flying-from-tree-to-tree lesson tomorrow and see how he gets on. I want him to be free as air . . . as free as—as a bird.'

In the middle of Great Aunt Angela's little square of lawn was a small tree, doing its best to be a tree in spite of being barbered and bobbed every spring and autumn. Still, if you really wanted to you could climb up into it and from there you could see almost over the top of the high hedge. However, Sam was not supposed to climb it for fear of falling down and hurting himself.

'Look, Fernando!' Sam cried. 'Watch me!' He made himself wings out of a corrugated cardboard carton and an old feather duster and tied them on at his wrists and shoulders. Zooming over the lawn he climbed up into the tree so rapidly that it did almost look as if he were flying. He stood on the topmost branch sweeping his wings up and down, and his wild free cries had a real echo of distance in them. It was as if all the journeys locked up inside him were crying out aloud against the high hedges and the closed gates. But Fernando Eagle shook his head and looked back over his shoulder longingly to Great Aunt Angela's kitchen.

'Blow!' thought Sam. 'He's not getting the idea. If only I had another tree . . . one's not enough for a proper tree-to-tree exercise.' An idea came to him, and he went into Great Aunt Angela's tiny tool-shed and brought out her all-aluminium-extendable-collapsible step-ladder and stood it close to the tree. He stuck it all over with pieces of hedge and fallen leaves.

'Look, Fernando!' he said, pointing at the tree. 'Tree! Tree! Get it?' Fernando pretended to scratch his ear with one foot while balancing on the other, and Sam was encouraged by this display of skill. He pointed to the step-ladder. 'Another tree!' he said slowly and clearly, though he had to admit, secretly, that it did not look very like a tree in spite of all his work. 'Another tree! Two trees! Now watch!' Waving his wings gracefully he climbed the step-ladder, stood there beautifully balanced and then leaped from the step-ladder into the top branches of Great Aunt Angela's tree. He did this supremely well . . . he really did look as if he were flying. But unfortunately Great Aunt Angela chose that moment to look through the kitchen window, just checking up.

'Sam!' she screamed. 'Oh Sam! Oh! Come down at once, you inconsiderate boy! What's got into you? Are you trying to drive me to my death?'

'I was teaching Fernando how to fly,' Sam began to explain, but it was no use. He was called untidy, dirty and dangerous, the sort of boy who would set a bad example to a pet.

'Fernando doesn't *need* to fly!' Great Aunt Angela declared. 'He doesn't *want* to fly. Look, you've made him hide his head under his wing, poor thing. And he's been a model bird all day. I was worried to begin with, he was so brightly coloured he looked a bit raffish, but his feathers are beginning to lose that flashy patchiness and settle down to a nice quiet grey.'

And so they were. Parts of him were about the same colour as Sam's school uniform.

'That shows he's happy!' said Great Aunt Angela with satisfaction. 'So don't upset him.'

Sam felt desperate. It seemed to him that if Fernando Eagle couldn't learn to fly, he, Sam, would live for ever behind high hedges and closed gates until all his journeys withered and died inside him. 'Go here! Go there! Up . . . up . . . away . . . awa.a.ay . . .' called the voices in his head and he thought Fernando Eagle must hear them too. But he didn't. He ate platefuls of bread and jam and grew neater and more school-uniformish day by day—taller too. Now he was just the same size as Sam himself.

Great Aunt Angela knitted him a little blue scarf and a blue woolly cap with a white tassel, and fussed over him more and more. It was as if Fernando was the real person in the house and

Sam just some sort of unnecessary ghost who had got in behind the high hedge by accident. One day when Sam and Fernando were on the lawn doing nothing much, Sam flapping his arms in a tired fashion and Fernando looking the other way, Great Aunt Angela came out of the house in her good going-out coat pushing her shopping trolley in front of her.

'Norton!' she called. 'Norr-ton! I'm going down to the supermarket. You may come with me if you like and push the trolley.'

Sam was astounded to hear Fernando Eagle reply in a very ordinary voice, as if he had been talking ever since he was hatched out of the egg, 'Yes Aunt Angela! I'd love to. Does Sam have to come as well?'

'Who's Sam?' the Great Aunt said. 'Some little imaginary friend of yours? Now, Norton, don't become too fanciful. Too much fancy is a very dangerous thing for a growing boy.'

'I will be careful, Auntie, I promise,' answered the foolish bird. 'I really will. May I push the trolley all the way to the shops?'

'Of course you may,' replied Great Aunt Angela graciously. 'You deserve a little treat. You've eaten up your greens and your bread and jam so well lately.'

Sam watched them as they set off down the drive. He felt lonely because, though he had never got on very well with Great Aunt Angela, she was the only relation he had. But more than that, he felt desperate for Fernando Eagle.

'One last chance!' he thought. 'One last chance for him to see that he doesn't have to stay here. He can fly away and be free.'

'Fernando!' he called. 'It's your last chance. You must fly. You must FLY.' He ran down the drive after them and all his imprisoned journeys rose up inside him like leaping flames. 'Like *this*, Fernando!' He held out his arms and the world turned under him. Aunt Angela carefully closed her gate but Sam went up over it and did not come down again. The air took him into itself. He, Sam, was the one to fly.

As if he had been flying for years he rose up higher than the high hedge and saw the whole street beyond—the traffic-lights winking at him and the shops behind the traffic-lights. He even thought he could see the pet shop man at the pet shop door.

'Up and away!' said a voice like a bell ringing in his head. He had often heard it before but never so clearly and now he could do what it told him to do. Up and away he went, between the painted roofs and the chimneys, frightening sparrows, scolded by startled starlings. Up and away, over the chimneys now, and suddenly all directions were possible for him.

The city looked at first like a game of noughts-and-crosses being played beneath him, and then like a great clockwork Christmas present, muttering to itself while lights flashed on and off.

'Up and away!' said the voice like a bell, and a new silvery voice whispered,

'The sea! The sea!'

'Are you surprised?' asked a third voice, but not in his head. This one came from beside him, and there was the pet shop man flying too. 'I saw your Aunt and Norton trembling together by the traffic-lights so I thought you must be up here somewhere.'

Sam thought of Norton and felt sad for the stay-at-home bird. 'I wanted him to be Fernando Eagle,' he said.

'Fernando Eagle never existed,' replied the pet shop man. 'Believe me, you were the eagle of your Great Aunt's house. There was no eagle space left for a bird to fit into. But there was a Norton space. ... a grey bread-and-jam-trolley-pushing space and he fitted in there exactly. He'll be very happy and so will your Great Aunt. Look! There they go.'

Far below like grey ants, Aunt Angela and Norton crawled back towards the front gate and locked it behind them, shutting out the dangerous clockwork city.

'The sea! The sea!' insisted the silver voice and Sam saw that he was indeed set free. Below him lay the world threaded with the bright tracks of a thousand possible journeys. The west wind came alongside him as he flew. A salt taste came into the air.

'You choose!' said the pet shop man. 'It's your first journey. I'll come as far as the beach with you to see you on your way. You'll meet other travellers, of course, but even when you don't you'll never be lonely, for a journey is all the companion a true traveller needs.'

So Sam flew off on the first of his great journeys. He was a boy with somewhere to go and able, at last, to go there, and as he flew the sun shone down on him and turned him from a boy in grey into a traveller of gold.

Gloves and Gardens

On one side of town Dido Digby's mother was hustling her into a taxi and giving her good advice.

'Give my love to Uncle Lupin, and whatever you do, keep your gloves on all the time. We don't want him to think we're weird, do we?'

'I'm not weird,' said Dido. 'I'm perfectly normal—except for THAT. He might think wearing gloves all the time is even more weird.'

'Well, keep them on anyway,' ordered her mother. 'Tell him you've got bad circulation or a rash—tell him you've got an allergy. Tell him anything but don't take them off. Now give me a kiss!'

Dido gave her mother a kiss and the newspaper and television men who were watching took loving pictures.

'Have a good trip round the world,' called Dido politely, and her mother suddenly laughed with happiness.

'Oh I shall, I shall. You'll be able to check up on me in the newspapers. I'm sure you'll enjoy it at Lupin's. Goodbye, darling.'

On the other side of the city where the houses began to stop and the country began to begin, Lupin Digby himself was waking up and remembering that this was the day his niece was coming to visit him.

'I must remember to wear my gloves the whole time,' he thought. 'Poor child, being sent to stay with an unknown uncle! It's only a little thing but it might alarm her. I'll hide it if I can.'

His morning paper was waiting for him in the box and when he had made himself a pot of tea and spread his toast with damson jam he went out into the garden as he always did, unless it was actually raining, and sat under the flowering gum with his back to the big flowerbed. The hollyhocks read the headlines over his shoulder.

Harriet Digby to sail around the world single-handed

Harriet was Dido's mother and Lupin's sister-in-law—a dark and dashing lady of a thousand parachute jumps, queen of the hang-gliders. She was in the *Guinness Book of Records* five times for having gone the furthest or the highest, or for being the only woman to get there at all. She made her living, and amused herself too, by getting into the *Guinness Book of Records*.

Lupin would have read a lot more about his sister-in-law but the red hollyhock, always the boldest one, bent over him like a sort of flowery giraffe and nudged him in a gentle but anxious way.

'All right, all right!' said Lupin, trying to take no notice, but the hollyhock rubbed its rough buds against him and he had to leave his paper and go and get his watering-can.

Lupin's garden was quite small but very beautiful with borders of pinks and catmint, blue and white cornflowers, scarlet poppies and white daisies. Behind these grew the freckled spires of foxgloves, pink and purple, blue delphiniums, and tall sunflowers with dark faces framed in bonnets of gold.

'Just time to get in a bit of work among the vegetables,' Lupin thought, watching the sun move across his little lawn. 'She's probably on the way now.' He took his hoe down to the rows of young corn and tender peas, lined the carrots up, spoke sternly to the radishes, and gently encouraged the peppers. He ate a stick of celery and a leaf of sorrel and picked the laterals out of some ambitious tomatoes. The wind was his companion but not always helpful. Sowing seeds carelessly, it puffed at a dandelion clock and Lupin counted the puffs.

'Two minutes to visitor time,' he decided. 'I'll go up now and I'll keep my gloves on. I'm sure that's the best thing to do, just to be on the safe side. Just in case!'

He reached the gate as the taxi was drawing up on the road outside. His blue-and-white gloves made him look as if he were carrying a big bunch of forget-me-nots.

The taxi stopped and a single passenger climbed out. She looked at Mr. Lupin and he looked back at her.

'Dido?' he asked. 'Is it Dido Digby?'

She smiled a little. 'Are you Uncle Lupin?'

'Lupin by name, and Lupin by nature,' he replied an
pointed to the pink and blue spikes that grew around hi
gate-posts and along the strip between his fence and the road.

'It's very pretty.' Dido looked at them out of eyes as dar
and rich as good compost. She was about ten years old, tall an
thin and pale and shy like a plant grown in the shadows bu
determined to get to the sunlight somehow. She wore a brow
coat with a velvet collar and thick woolly gloves though the da
was quite warm.

'Come in! Let me carry your bag.' Lupin bustled aroun
her. 'It's nice to see you. We haven't met since you were th
merest baby in a little white dress and little white boots an
little white gloves. Now you're grown from top to toe. An
how's your mother?'

'Very adventurous,' Dido said. 'She's going to sail aroun
the world in a new sort of catamaran. That's the sort of mothe
she's turned out to be. Always adventurous.'

'She was adventurous as a girl when she lived next door t
us,' Lupin recalled. 'Swinging from trees, sliding down th
garage roof, scrambling, tumbling, rambling, speeding on he
bike. It must be a lot of fun having her as a mother.'

'It's exciting having her as a mother, but I think it's borin
for her having me as a daughter.' Dido sighed. 'When sh
wants to go out and have adventures I'm always there having t
be looked after. She wants things to happen quickly all th
time, but I like them to happen slowly. Sometimes I even lik
them to stand still so that I can look at them properly.'

Lupin took Dido upstairs and showed her her bedroom
with its blue quilt and white pillow and the vase of red roses.

'Hang up your coat and unpack. Then come downstairs fo
a cup of tea,' he told her. 'I'll go and put the kettle on.'

Lupin ran into the kitchen and took off his blue-and-whit
gardening gloves. He quickly made sandwiches with a tomato
grown in his little glasshouse—a tomato so big it made four
whole sandwiches. The water boiled and he was just setting th

98

cups out when he heard Dido in the hall. Quickly he put his gloves back on, and by the time Dido came into the kitchen Lupin's secret was safely hidden away in blue-and-white check. When he offered her a cup of tea it seemed he was offering her a handful of forget-me-nots with it.

When Dido put out her hand to take the cup, Lupin couldn't help noticing that she was wearing gloves, too— different gloves from the ones she had worn earlier—pink cotton ones with no pattern. They looked like skin. They were person-coloured gloves. Lupin gave her a curious look while Dido, for her part, stared hard at his gardening gloves, and then raised her dark eyes to his face to study the lines there, as if they might be a map showing where treasure was hidden.

'Let's have our tea in the garden,' said Lupin and out they went carrying their tea in their gloved hands. The sun had gone in but in Lupin's garden it always seemed to be fine weather, with the blue of the delphiniums and larkspurs, and the sunflowers filling the air with their own special sunshine.

As Dido stepped out through the door a strange thing happened. The whole garden sighed and rustled as if a little wind had blown over it. Yet Lupin felt no breath of wind on his face. The air was still but suddenly excited as if it were waiting for something to happen. Within this stillness the garden whispered and murmured and tapped and ticked like a green clock keeping a special old garden time of its own. The red hollyhock bent itself down, but not to Lupin. It bent its crimson flowers and rough buds down to Dido.

'Do they often do that?' Dido asked, surprised.

'Not often!' Lupin looked at his hollyhock in astonishment. 'Sometimes, when it thinks it wants a drink of water!'

'This is a *real* garden,' Dido said, touching the hollyhock very gently. 'Better than a park or one of those prize-winning gardens you see in books. Once I had a window-box but I had to take it down.'

'Didn't anything grow?' asked Lupin sympathetically. 'That sometimes happens. Gardening isn't easy, you know.'

'Things grew too much,' Dido explained. 'The window got

covered over with beans and a great forest of parsley. You must do a lot of gardening, Uncle Lupin.'

'It's what I do most of,' agreed Lupin. 'My own, and other people's. I'm good at it too—you might say I've got green . . .' he stopped.

'Green . . . ?' Dido's voice asked a question.

'Green—green apples,' stammered Lupin. 'I've got several apple trees, and lots of green apples on them.' He looked shyly down at his gardening gloves.

They spent the rest of the morning planting out young lettuces and thinning the green apples which weighed down the branches of the old trees. As they worked, Lupin watched Dido's pink gloves out of the corner of his eyes—the very colour of good soil just watered. Dido watched Lupin's blue-and-white check gloves with her compost-coloured eyes.

'Do you always wear gloves, Dido?' asked Lupin boldly.

'Yes, Uncle Lupin. Do you?' Dido replied.

'Mostly I do,' replied Lupin calmly. 'I don't feel dressed without my gardening gloves.'

When Dido went to bed that night her pillow smelled of Lupin's own lavender. While she was asleep Lupin looked in at the door to check that she was comfortable. He had enjoyed her company in his garden that afternoon.

'A niece after my own heart,' he muttered. 'She'd be wasted going around the world on a catamaran or a dogomaran or whatever and suchlike. I'll teach her to be a gardener while she stays with me and then she'll have a trade wherever she goes. You'll never starve if you can grow a cabbage or a potato and you'll never be lonely if you can grow a hollyhock. That's what I say.'

He looked at Dido's hands on her blue quilt. Even asleep she was wearing her pink gloves.

Overnight the clouds rolled away. Dido, in her pink gloves, woke up and lay in the honey-coloured morning silence. Lupin woke up in a room flickering with light and shade as the sunshine shone in through the long, leafy, runaway stems of pineapple sage that crossed his window.

It was a real green-apple day—sharp, clean, very crisp, with a greenish light in the air as if the hills were using the sky for their looking-glass.

'Breakfast in the garden?' asked Lupin.

'Of course,' answered Dido, and they sat out in cane chairs eating their toast and honey.

'Will we garden today?' Dido asked. 'I'd like to learn about some flowers.'

As she spoke, not only the red hollyhock but the white one, and the pink one too, put their heads over her shoulder and brushed her cheek with their flowers.

'Look at that!' cried Lupin wonderingly and . . .

'Look at *that*!' he cried again when they went down to check on yesterday's lettuces. The ones that Dido had planted were twice as big as Lupins, almost ready to eat.

'Dido,' Lupin cried, 'you must be a born gardener.'

'I thought it was that,' Dido said. 'But my mother doesn't like it. She thinks it's strange.'

'A good strangeness!' said Lupin encouragingly. 'It's every bit as good to stay at home and grow a garden, as to travel around the world in a catamaran or a cataramouse or whatever she calls it.'

'You really think so?' asked Dido shyly.

'Of course I do,' cried Lupin. Dido smiled. She began to take off her gloves. Lupin began to take his off too.

'Don't be scared, will you?' they said anxiously each to the other. They held their hands closed into fists for a moment, the thumbs and fingers tucked in. Then they opened their hands wide in the soft garden air.

Dido's thumbs and fingers were green—soft, mossy green fingers, old on such young hands, secret mossy thumbs, with nails of green pearl. Lupin's thumbs and fingers were green too—green as oak leaves in the spring, young fingers on old hands, thumbs that looked newly-grown, fresh and hopeful, unfurling like fern fronds.

'Touch the ground—touch the ground with your bare hand,' whispered Lupin.

'I'm not supposed to,' Dido whispered back, but she bent and crumpled a tiny clod of dirt between green thumb and green fingers.

Leaves stitched the ground and tiny starry flowers blossomed, their hearts like pin-heads of gold.

'There never were such green fingers!' Lupin said, while the garden sighed around them. 'Some day you'll have a garden of your own. But in the meantime we'll share this one.'

'Will we do flowers this morning?' Dido asked eagerly.

'Flowers this morning,' Lupin promised, 'and beans this afternoon and this evening we'll concentrate on water-melons. We could even manage pineapples and bananas between us.'

The two gardeners began planning their garden on that crisp green-apple day, and in their two laps their green fingers lay curled and waiting for the moment when they would touch the soil and set things growing by their green magic.

The Singing Bus Queue

Little Jim was the last and least person in the weekday bu
queue. But one morning while he was standing there waitin
for the bus an unexpected song came into his head. It was th
sort of song that needed to be sung at once, so Jim lifted up hi
voice and sang it.

The other people at the bus stop all tried to take no notice o
his song. They were Mrs. Mavis Mincham with her re
shopping-bag, the Tufnell twins who wore everything match
ing, Mr. Woolf with his hat pulled down, his collar turned up
and his buttons buttoned from top to toe, Comrade Wilkins th
revolutionary poet and Trishie Fisher who needed a haircut.

When little Jim had finished his song he sang it all ove
again.

'Kids these days!' snapped Mrs. Mavis Mincham. 'The
think they can get away with anything. But that's a very catch
song.'

And before she quite knew what she was doing she was singing it too. Mr. Woolf joined in in a singular tenor voice quite surprising in one so tall, while Comrade Wilkins, who seemed so wispy and thin, proved to have a great booming voice, big enough to fill a Town Hall and a couple of cathedrals. The Tufnell twins chimed in with practised harmony, every note matching, and at last even Trishie Fisher couldn't resist singing too, though she was thirteen and anxious not to seem childish.

When they had finished the song they all laughed and shook hands. Then they sang it again.

Not everyone liked the singing.

'People should stand quietly and neatly while waiting for a bus,' said Major Hannibal, a military man who lived nearby.

'Suppose everyone went around singing and laughing and shaking hands . . . why, pandemonium! Pure anarchy!'

The bus queue began to sing 'Frère Jacques' as a round. They got it right straight off.

'Things are not what they ought to be,' said Major Hanni
bal darkly.

In the days that followed, the bus queue sang every morn
ing, and they sang better and better. At first passers-by looked
and grinned, but then they began to stop and stand and listen.

'What did I tell you?' muttered Major Hannibal to hi
neighbour, Mr. Hyrax. 'There ought to be a law against it.'

To begin with the bus queue sang simple rounds, and par
songs, but as they became better and better, they sang canon
and catches, cantatas and canticles, and all kinds of choruses
People began to come from far away to these morning concerts
dozens of music lovers, hundreds of music lovers, tripping o
jogging or pedalling on bicycles, talking about yesterday'
concert, guessing about what would be sung that morning
many of them bringing their breakfast with them. The bu
queue would sing some serenade or anthem, follow it with
round, or perhaps the song they had first thought of, and the
wind up with selections of well known operas arranged fo
seven voices. Then the bus would come and they would all ge
on to it to be driven off to work or school. Once they were o
the bus they stopped being a singing bus queue and became jus
ordinary passengers.

One morning as the music lovers collected on the footpath
full of cornflakes, toast and anticipation, a policema
appeared.

'Move along there!' he cried. 'You're blocking the publi
thoroughfare. This is unlawful assembly and it's got to stop.'

'I phoned the police,' whispered Major Hannibal to Mr
Hyrax. 'I thought they ought to know what's going on aroun
here.'

'Move along there!' the policeman said in a stern lega
voice, but at that moment the bus queue began to sing
wonderful Italian madrigal three hundred years old, arranged
for seven voices. Trishie Fisher sang sweet as a flute, the
Tufnell twins together made up one very rich unusual voice
Mrs. Mavis Mincham's golden contralto notes fell from her lips
like glowing pearls, while Comrade Wilkins vibrated like an

106

orchestra made up entirely of tubas and bassoons. Little Jim piped like a piccolo and as for Mr. Woolf—his tenor was as mellow and kind as the last sunny apple on autumn's apple tree.

The policeman was utterly enchanted. In the flash of an eye he changed from being a policeman to being a music lover and stood listening until the bus came.

Well, the next morning, as the music lovers assembled, two police cars drew up and four policemen got out and began to move the crowd along. But as soon as the bus queue started singing the policemen became rigid with delight and listened with everyone else, for the bus queue were singing a fine old song, 'If you want to know the time, ask a policeman', in close harmony. No officer of the law could be insensible to such a delicate compliment and the bus queue concert went on undisturbed.

'Right!' muttered Major Hannibal. 'I'll fix them this time.' He phoned the police station for the third time and the following morning a special contingent of policemen were dispatched to break up the bus queue concert. These policemen were not only very fierce but were all selected because they were tone-deaf and therefore did not enjoy music. The wonderful harmony and counterpoint of the singing bus queue could not make any impression on these constabulary ears. The unlawful assembly of music lovers was broken up, and the bus queue audience was driven home by threats of prosecution and arrest.

'That fixes that!' cried Major Hannibal triumphantly.

But there was something Major Hannibal did not understand about the singing bus queue. They sang for the sake of the song not the listeners. So next morning even though the street was empty of any audience, except for Major Hannibal and Mr. Hyrax leaning on their triumphant gateposts and a few workers hurrying by, the bus queue sang a most tender and moving septet so beautifully that a single teardrop, clear as spring water, squeezed itself out of one of Mr. Hyrax's little blue eyes and trickled down beside his little red nose.

When he saw this Major Hannibal was overcome with fury. He went back to his telephone and phoned a councillor, Mrs.

Evadne Squills. She was particularly interested in civic by-laws and always thought you couldn't have enough of them. A few days after this conversation Mrs. Mavis Mincham turned up at the bus stop, red shopping-bag and all complete, and saw at once that a new notice had been put up beside the bus time-table. 'It is forbidden to sing while waiting for the bus under By-law 10007. Violators of this by-law will be punished with the utmost severity. Those failing to comply with this official directive will be put straight into the Black Prison for six months at least, so watch it!'

It was signed by Evadne Squills, Councillor with Special Responsibility for By-laws.

'Huh!' snorted Mrs. Mavis Mincham. 'That Evadne Squills! I remember her when she was a prefect at school always nosing and bossing. But I didn't taken any notice of her then, and I won't now.' She started in on a few warming-up exercises.

When Comrade Wilkins saw the notice he snorted too. 'Typical!' he cried. 'Trying to deprive the man in the street of his rights. Just as well there are people like me around prepared to combat bourgeois repression.'

When Mr. Woolf saw the notice he said nothing but he pulled his coat collar down and tilted his hat up in a very defiant gesture while the Tufnell twins elevated their matching noses into the air at exactly matching angles.

'What cheek!' the twins said as one Tufnell.

'Gosh!' exclaimed Trishie Fisher. 'Isn't that typical! Grown-ups think they've got to stop people enjoying themselves no matter what. Well, that won't stop me.'

'Let's sing now!' said little Jim and led the way into a rousing sea shanty.

Major Hannibal was out at his gate in a moment. 'It's illegal,' he shouted in his parade-ground-Sergeant-Major voice. 'Now you ghastly lot—stop that caterwauling and cacophony.' But the bus queue took no notice of his commandments. They merely swung into a very sarcastic rendering of 'The galloping major'.

'Right!' said the Major, belting back indoors to ring the police-station and order out the special Tone-Deaf Squad. 'Them that dies will be the lucky ones!'

In spite of unlawful assembly and strict by-laws people still stopped to listen to the fiery songs of defiance the bus queue was singing with so much fervour and feeling. They shouted and cheered as the bus queue sang seven national anthems one after the other and the Tone-Deaf Squad could hardly get to the bus stop through the crowd of excited music lovers.

'Silence in the name of the law!' shouted the tone-deaf policemen. 'You are violating By-law 10007 and unless you stop you will be put in the Black Prison for six months at least. Take notice!'

But the bus queue did not take notice. Instead they sang immediately a wonderful requiem so sorrowful, so noble that all the music lovers began to weep and even the tone-deaf policemen were harrowed by a mysterious sadness they could not explain. However, being tone-deaf they could not be diverted from their judicial duty and the whole bus queue was arrested at once. Singing they were carried through the streets in the police van, singing they were put into seven separate cells. Only then did they become silent.

Being in prison while awaiting their court cases wasn't too bad. They were given beans on toast for lunch and a plain but nourishing stew for dinner. Yet somehow the bus queue prisoners made the prison guards and warders feel rather creepy. They sat, all seven of them, in their cells quite silent, looking neither right nor left.

'They look as if they've gone to sleep sitting up,' said one warder.

'But their eyes are open,' said a second.

'Their eyes are open and shining,' said a third. 'Shining like the eyes of outer space monsters.'

'Well, they're not monsters,' said the first warder. 'They're just common or garden prisoners, wretched violators of by-laws. But they're a very creepy lot, I must say,' he added.

Darkness fell over the city. Lights twinkled below, sta[rs]
twinkled above. At eight o'clock the prisoners in the Blac[k]
Prison had their cell lights turned off for their own good.

'Honestly,' said one warder to another, 'if people wou[ld]
only have a few early nights a lot of our troubles would be ove[r.]
A lot of law-breaking is due to late hours.'

'Have you noticed those bus queue prisoners?' said [a]
watchman. 'I had a peep in at them, doing my rounds y[ou]
know, and they're all just sitting there looking neither right n[or]
left.'

'Eyes still shining?' asked the third warder nervously.

'Like polished coins!' the watchman said poetically. 'I'[ve]
never seen silver eyes before and I don't like them.'

The city twinkled up and the stars twinkled down. At fir[st]
the city was brighter but then, one by one, the house ligh[ts]
went out and the moon rose and the sky became enormous, o[ld]
and mysterious, while the city shrank and became smaller a[nd]
more unsure of itself.

At midnight exactly a moonbeam slid through the barre[d]
window of a cell in the Black Prison. It fell on little Jim ar[d]
turned him to a boy of silver with silver eyes.

Little Jim stood up and sang. It was a song that sudden[ly]
happened to come to him, and it needed to be sung.

Mr. Woolf heard Jim's note through the thick stone wa[ll]
and he joined in. Beyond him Mrs. Mavis Mincham opened h[er]
mouth and sang in a voice that she had never actually use[d]
before. The Tufnell twins had been shut up in separate (thoug[h]
matching) cells and yet they came into the song together, just [as]
if they had planned it. Comrade Wilkins' voice filled his ce[ll]
and overflowed next door, filling Trishie Fisher's too, whi[le]
she, for her part, sang out as clear as an evening blackbird[.]

In the staffroom the warders and watchmen fell silent f[or]
the Black Prison was vibrating with the sound.

Trishie sang a very high sweet note and the warders' mil[k]
jug broke. The Tufnell twins sang a matching tone and th[e]
prison staffroom window flew open, wide to the moonl[it]
night.

Now, in their separate cells, little Jim and Trishie Fisher sang together. Their voices rose higher and higher, shrill but still sweet. A cobweb of silver cracks suddenly sprang out all over the Black Prison. Higher still, and all the dogs in town joined in with a melancholy harmony of their own. Higher, to the very brink of hearing, and the silver cobweb widened and spread. One last long note so high it could be felt but not heard—and the Black Prison began to crumble away. Its tall towers bowed, its walls split and parted. Its windows fell out and its doors fell open. And somehow all the roaring of its fall was part of the song. Out through the tumble and totterment, the falling prison parting before them in a wave of stone and plaster, marched the singing bus queue. Behind them, led out of ruin to safety by the song, came the dazed watchmen and the warders.

Standing on the hilltop they all sang together and after a while the whole city joined in too, and possibly, even the moon and the stars. . . . the 'G' type stars, the white dwarfs, the red giants and exploded supergiants, the comets and the quasars, the planets and the pulsars. Only the black holes were silent for no sound could ever escape their improbable surfaces.

And then the sun came up and everyone went to bed or to work, whichever appealed to them most after a whole night of singing.

By-law 10007 was cancelled and the Tone-Deaf Squad were sent around to take down notices forbidding singing at bus-stops. Mrs. Evadne Squills, not to be done out of a by-law, replaced it with By-law 10008 which suggested that people should sing, not only at bus-stops, but in supermarkets, on street corners, outside cinemas, theatres and other places where queues were likely to form or where people liked to stand around.

The Black Prison was put up again, but it was now a music school and any municipal malefactors or miscreants who got taken there were taught to play a musical instrument or how to sing rounds. This mostly turned them from a life of crime, and those villains who remained unrepentant were so dismayed that they left town and never came back.

As for the bus queue that had started it all—of course the went on getting better and better, all eight of them.

Eight of them?

Well, you see, the morning after they had escaped from ja Major Hannibal, who had a perfectly good car in his garage came over and stood in the queue, too.

'Thought I'd take the bus today,' he said. And when the sang he sang too in a fine military baritone.

'After all,' he said to Mr. Hyrax, 'if you can't beat 'em, joi 'em.'

And soon after that he learned to play the trombone. Bu that's another story.

The Devil and the Corner Grocer

1 *A Pilot Project for a Corner Grocery*

One sparkling day when the sky was tender blue and speckled with innocent white clouds a travelling salesman suddenly appeared on the corner opposite the new supermarket.

The supermarket was busy with lots of customers pushing the supermarket trolleys around and lining up at the check-out counters but they did not notice the Traveller and he did not cross the road to join them. He walked on with a curious limping step, his traveller's case banging against his knee until he was opposite Mr. Philpott's corner grocery.

It was here that he chose to cross the road.

The corner grocery was one of those shops that sell a little of most useful things, one of those small shops that seem to have been there for ever.

'I thought I'd call in . . . show you some of the lines my firm is promoting this season,' the Traveller said, his shiny eyes flickering around the shop which was empty except for himself and Mr. Philpott. The groceries stirred uneasily on their shelves when his sharp eye fell on them. 'How's business?'

'Not too good,' said Mr. Philpott. 'Not since the supermarket opened.'

'Things tough?' asked the Traveller, still looking around the corner grocery in a very measuring way.

'Could be better,' admitted Mr. Philpott. 'You're the first traveller that's looked in on me for a while. In fact, between you and me, you're the first person to come through that door so far this morning. If things don't look up in the next day or two I'm thinking of closing the shop.'

'Oh don't do that,' the Traveller cried. 'Look, I've a new line here that my company is trying out in a few selected areas—a pilot scheme! I was told to offer it to a few people such as yourself and to follow it up, just to see how it goes.'

He opened his traveller's bag and produced several glass jars, all with typewritten labels. They were very pretty, each one filled with what looked like coloured salt. He set them out along the edge of the counter where they sparkled like jewels—red, blue, green, yellow, silver and purple. Mr. Philpott read the labels carefully, pushing his spectacles up on his nose to do so, while the Traveller watched him. He had black curls, this Traveller, worn long on a lumpy forehead, and a thin smile. 'I know all about *you*,' said that smile. 'You've got no secrets from *me*.'

Mr. Philpott looked up from reading the labels. 'Sound like a joke to me,' he said reproachfully. 'I wasn't born yesterday!'

The Traveller looked very hurt. 'It's a *new* line, I tell you,' he said. 'I'm not surprised you're a bit taken aback, but I promise you—years of research have gone into this little lot. We don't intend selling it through the supermarkets because we want it presented with sincerity, the personal touch.'

Mr. Philpott was impressed after all. 'Very well, I'll give it a go,' he said. 'Business can't be any worse than it is now. How much do I charge?'

'Penny a dose,' said the Traveller. 'Make 'em drink it here. A teaspoonful in water will do it, and each dose lasts ten days.'

'I won't make make my fortune that way,' Mr. Philpott said. 'Still if everyone who buys a dose buys a bag of oatmeal too—or a packet of chocolate biscuits, I won't complain. By the way—what was the name of your firm again?'

'Domdaniel Productions,' the Traveller replied promptly. 'A branch of the Pandemonium Group! Do you know it?'

'I don't think I do exactly,' said Mr. Philpott looking puzzled.

'A new firm is it?'

'Very old really,' the Traveller replied softly. 'We've been around for a long time—well, forever you know, doing steady business in our own way. I'll call in a few days and see how the line's going.'

He limped as he minced out of the shop.

'Bit stiff?' asked Mr. Philpott sympathetically.

'Oh no—just new shoes. They take a bit of breaking in and until they're broken, they're very hard on the hoofs.'

'The hoofs?' Mr. Philpott looked cautious.

'I mean to say the feet,' said the Traveller with a smile over his shoulder, a terrible thin smile. 'The feet, I repeat!'

'Goodbye then,' said Mr. Philpott thoughtfully.

2 *Instant Courage*

The first person to come into the shop after the Traveller had gone was a very nervous fat boy called Damian Bullock. The most notable thing about Damian, apart from his fatness, was his constant terror. He was frightened of dogs, roosters, spiders, and mice. He was frightened of most loud noises and certain soft ones, of boys bigger than he was, the same size as he was and slightly smaller ones too. He was frightened of girls, teachers, his own father, thunder and lightning. He came into Mr. Philpott's shop because he could see a very tough redheaded boy known as Copper Candle lurking down the road with his gang and Damian was naturally terrified of Copper Candle.

'Hello Damian,' said Mr. Philpott heartily, and Damian winced to hear his name spoken so loudly.

'I'll have a jelly baby,' he whispered.

'Nothing easier,' replied Mr. Philpott. He looked at the glass jars on his counter—particularly a certain rose-red one—and then he looked back at poor, quavering Damian. 'Why not give it a go?' he thought.

'I've got a new product here that might interest you,' he said. 'You know you can buy instant coffee, instant soup, instant mashed potato and so on. Well, I have a new range of instants here—Instant Beauty for instance, Instant Youth, Instant Courage, Instant . . .'

'Did you say Instant Courage?' Damian asked.

115

'Penny a dose,' Mr. Philpott said. 'Very reasonable reall It lasts ten days.'

'I've got a penny,' Damian mumbled. He looked terrifie again. 'What does it taste like?'

'I'll fetch a glass of water,' Mr. Philpott offered helpfully. teaspoon of the rose-red powder dissolved at once with musical fizzing, very refreshing to hear. The water turned pin and sparkled mysteriously. Damian looked frightened.

'You have first taste,' he said cautiously.

'Oh I'm brave enough for my own good,' Mr. Philpo replied.

'Go on—it won't bite you.'

Damian shuddered at the word 'bite' but he picked up th mysteriously sparkling drink, sipped it, then swallowed down quite easily, so it must have tasted nice. Instantl Damian became mysterious and sparkling too. Mr. Philpo watched with keen interest. 'How was that? Not too bad?' h asked anxiously.

'Really good,' said Damian. 'It works, Mr. Philpott.' H voice was bright and cool and amused. 'Well, I'd better b going. Copper Candle and his gang are waiting to beat me u just down the road, but I'm not scared of them any more.'

And off he went swinging his school satchel. A momen later the sound of a terrible fight broke out down the road. M Philpott looked at his Domdaniel Instants with respect an alarm. 'Dear me!' he thought. 'I only hope I didn't give him a overdose.'

3 *Instant Beauty*

The next customer was Alona Perry, a thin freckled girl with crooked nose. Mr. Philpott knew something was wrong once, for Alona was usually one of the world's smilers but toda her smile looked as if it was being pushed on stage against i will, not wanting to be seen at all.

'A loaf of wholemeal bread,' Alona said. 'That's all I want today, Mr. Philpott.'

'If that's really all you want, your luck's in,' Mr. Philpott replied, reaching for a loaf from his bread shelf. 'I mean you're lucky to want so little.'

'It's not really all I want,' Alona said. 'But the rest of what I want can't be bought at shops, Mr. Philpott.'

'Well, you never know—these days,' Mr Philpott murmured vaguely, looking at his row of Domdaniel Instants. 'What did you have in mind?'

'Oh nothing much—just long golden hair and a skin like rose petals, straight nose, a wildly beautiful figure and eyes like pansies with the dew on them.' Alona sighed gloomily. 'Here I am, trying to be an actress, and all the plays have beautiful heroines. It's very hard. I never *look* right for the part.'

'In that case what you need is a dose of Instant Beauty,' Mr. Philpott declared boldly, 'though mind you, Alona, if it's any comfort to you I think you look O.K. the way you are now, and so does that young Jack Thingummy down the road.'

'Did you say Instant Beauty?' asked Alona, ignoring young Jack Thingummy. 'Look, the best face-cream in the world isn't going to straighten out my nose, let alone curl my hair and make me tall and graceful.'

'It's not a face-cream. It's a dose,' Mr. Philpott said. 'One teaspoonful in water. I sold young Damian Bullock a dose of Instant Courage and it worked like a charm.'

'I suppose that's why he's down the road being beaten up by Copper Candle and his gang instead of hiding behind gateposts the way he usually does,' Alona cried scornfully, and then she suddenly laughed. 'All right Mr. Philpott—let me try your Instant Beauty.'

The purple powder dissolved with a lavender sparkle, smelling of spring and flowers. Alona did not hesitate. She drank it down quickly. Immediately she became so beautiful she cast a kind of silvery light that reflected off all the shiny things in the shop. Tin openers, kitchen scissors, and aluminium frying pans shimmered like planets in the light of a

silver sun. Yet curiously enough, though now as beautiful as
goddess and as dark and mysterious as two o'clock in th
morning, Alona was still herself, looking out with her speci
Alona expression through eyelashes, thick, soft and long. '
has actually worked, hasn't it?' she cried in thrilling tones. '
can see myself reflected in your eyes. Yippee! I am . . . I A
absolutely beautiful. I actually look like a heroine, I *really* loo
like an actress. Thank you, thank you, Mr. Philpott.'

'That'll be a penny,' Mr. Philpott said firmly.

'Money well spent!' Alona answered enthusiastically, 'an
I'll have that wholemeal bread I mentioned . . . oh and som
sardines, a bag of brown rice, soap powder, a refill for a sponge
mop and a packet of frozen peas.'

'Straightaway!' said Mr. Philpott, delighted at this goo
sale, even though it seemed unnatural to be wrapping
sponge-mop for someone as beautiful as Alona was now. M
Philpott felt he should be giving her grapes, cherries, and
bottle of white wine in a basket of golden straw.

'A million thanks, Mr. Philpott,' Alona said, shining like
summer moon.

'All part of the corner grocery service!' replied Mr. Philpo
as if he'd sold Instant Beauty in his shop for years.

A little later, when Alona had gone, he looked sternly at th
Domdaniel Instants sparkling smugly on his counter.

'Clever, aren't you!' he said to them. 'Dangerous too!' H
picked up the blue one and studied it closely, and his frow
began to clear.

'If this one works the way the label says it will, I don't hav
much to worry about,' he muttered. 'And I don't see why
shouldn't . . . the others did. After all, it's one thing to b
clever, but a totally different thing to be wise.'

He began to put his jars away on a shelf behind his counte
and did not see a shadow fall across his doorway. A tall
hunchbacked figure came silently up to the counter, looked
Mr. Philpott's busy back for nearly a minute, and then at las
spoke to him. 'Excuse me,' it said, 'but may I have a word wit
you?'

118

4 *Jack Misses Alona's Freckles*

Alona went down the street, a shimmering rainbow in the clear air.

'Alona, is that you?' said kind Mrs. Jackson blinking at her. Goodness, I nearly walked right past. You do look WELL, and you're getting to look like that pretty aunt of yours who went in for hairdressing.'

Alona smiled, and an impressionable young man going past on a bicycle steered into the gutter and fell over his own handlebars. Further down the road she passed Damian Bullock fighting Copper Candle and his gang singlehanded. He was tremendously brave but, as he was not very good at fighting, he was bruised and bloody from head to toe. The fighting stopped as Alona walked past. There was a feeling of confusion in the air. What with Damian turning brave and Alona becoming beautiful, people didn't know where they were.

'You are quite amazingly beautiful,' said a polite voice from her elbow, and there beside her was a person she had never met before, a person with a bumpy forehead, black woolly curls and a curiously unpleasant smile. 'See how people are staring at you. Goodness me . . . with beauty like yours you could be queen of the town—of the whole country, of the world, even. Have you thought of that?'

'I haven't had time to think of anything much,' Alona replied. 'I've only just become as beautiful as this, but I won't have time to be queen of anything. I'm going to be an actress and you have to work hard for that. Being beautiful is a big help, of course, but you still have to work at it.'

'Why bother?' asked the stranger. 'You can have the riches, the applause, the power . . . all that, without having to be an actress.'

Alona frowned at him. 'But I WANT to be an actress,' she said.

'I see,' he answered. 'What a pity . . . but perhaps you'll change your mind. Think about it!' And he drifted back towards the Damian Bullock–Copper Candle fight.

'Who'd want to be a queen if they could be an actress?' thought Alona. She saw her friend Jack in the distance. 'He's going to be surprised,' she thought and chuckled a little, going on her radiant way, her path marked by swerving cars, starts and sudden silences. Only Jack was not entirely impressed.

'What have you done with your freckles?' he cried. 'I really liked them.'

5 *Meanwhile, Back at the Grocery* . . .

Mr. Philpott faced his new customer with a feeling of slight alarm. The goods on the shelves seemed to peer down eagerly as if they looked forward to seeing Mr. Philpott in trouble. He glanced at them reproachfully—he had always looked after them well and yet now he felt they were ganging up on him with this strange customer. For there *was* something strange about the man before him, even though he wore a white business suit and a pink-and-green striped tie. His eyes were like gold coins with holes in the middle of them, and held you in a remarkably steadfast, piercing gaze.

'What can I do for you?' Mr. Philpott asked politely.

'You have just had a visit from an unusual travelling salesman,' the Stranger said.

'Yes, about half an hour ago,' said Mr. Philpott.

'Did you notice his feet?' asked the Stranger.

'His shoes were hurting him,' Mr. Philpott replied cautiously.

'Did he try to sell you anything?' the Stranger asked again.

'As a matter of fact, he did,' Mr. Philpott admitted, 'but very cheaply—a mere nominal sum. It's a sort of pilot project.'

'Instant Strength?' The Stranger arched his eyebrows.

'Instant Strength, Instant Beauty, Instant Wisdom. . .' nodded Mr. Philpott. 'All that sort of instant stuff. Just what I needed to give my stock a lift. What with the supermarket opening down the road, business has been a bit quiet lately.'

The Stranger placed his hands on the counter and studied Mr. Philpott with his golden eyes. 'I'm afraid you've been tricked,' he said at last. 'Those mixtures are highly dangerous and you shouldn't be selling them.'

'I've tried them out on two people already,' Mr. Philpott argued, 'and believe me they were perfectly satisfied. No complaints at all.'

'But beauty and courage aren't meant to be instant,' the Stranger declared. 'People are meant to grow into them, not get them all at once. And I should know because I represent the group that invented beauty and courage and all the others—Paradise Enterprises. That Domdaniel group had no right to take our products, turn them into instant ones, and market them like that—they're pirating our products. They'll do anything to cause trouble—that Domdaniel group. And it *will* cause trouble. Everyone in this town will be out of balance with the rest of the world. If they become beautiful and strong and courageous so easily they'll become greedy and ambitious for power. Mr. Philpott, I suggest you hand over these Instants to me. They'll do no more harm once they're in my pocket.'

'Goodness—what a suggestion!' Mr. Philpott said. 'Why, for all I know you're from the supermarket down the road. I'm not going to hand over my goods just like that. For one thing I don't want to disappoint my customers, and for another I can see these items are going to be good for trade.'

'I advise you, very strongly, to give them to me,' the Stranger repeated. Mr Philpott looked into the dark centres of his golden eyes and thought for a moment he was travelling down two long black tunnels and seeing, far away at the end of them, a sky full of stars. Then Mr. Philpott blinked, or perhaps the Stranger blinked, and the shop grew real again and so did the Stranger, standing there with his head sunk down beneath his high shoulders.

'I'm warning you for your own good,' the Stranger said.

'I'd rather hang on to them for the present,' Mr. Philpott said firmly, 'and give them a go.'

'You have been warned,' exclaimed the Stranger sternly.

'Thank you!' said Mr. Philpott humbly. 'It's good of you to take the trouble. I really appreciate it.' But the Stranger left going so swiftly he seemed to leave the shop and even the street in a single stride, for a moment later he was nowhere to be seen.

'*His* shoes weren't too tight anyway,' Mr. Philpott thought 'On the other hand he looked very round-shouldered. Pity! Oh well, it would be a dull world if we were all the same.'

He closed up his shop for the night, but word of the new pilot scheme must have got around because next morning he found a small queue outside his corner grocery door—something he couldn't remember ever having happened previously, even in the days before the supermarket came along

6 *Satisfied Customers*

It turned out to be the busiest day Mr. Philpott could remember in thirty-five years of corner grocerying. First of all a Council bulldozer broke down in front of his shop which mean' that there were a lot of Council bulldozer men standing around and shaking their heads despondently. And then there was an early morning grocery queue to deal with. One after another five young women inquired about doses of Instant Beauty. One by one they were transformed into veritable goddesses—one fair, one dark, two brown and one red. This caused the bulldozer men to forget about the bulldozer for about ten minutes at the very least. During this time Damian Bullock came in with a nose as red and swollen as a boiled sausage.

'Do you want Instant Beauty, too?' asked Mr. Philpott. 'You look as if you could do with it more than most.'

'The thing is,' explained Damian, 'I'm not scared of Copper Candle and his gang any more, but I can't stop them beating me up. Being a coward made me miserable in a lot of ways, but it kept me safe. Have you got anything to go with Instant Courage? Something that might save me from being beaten up again. Can't you make me invisible or something?'

'No sense in being brave if no one can actually see you being brave,' Mr. Philpott said sensibly. He looked along his line of Domdaniel Instants. 'How about this green one . . . Instant Strength. That might do the trick.'

Damian tried it, and immediately became extremely strong . . . so strong that without the slightest hesitation he marched out on to the road and began to push the bulldozer down towards the Council Bulldozer Repair Workshop which was on his way to school anyway. The bulldozer men were electrified for the second time that morning and cast curious glances in at the corner grocery.

Mr. Philpott watched Damian go with a smile on his grocerly countenance. 'Another satisfied customer!' he murmured.

The next customer to be satisfied was a young man called Joe Brassbound who had some very hard exams to sit the next day. His rich aunt wanted him to be a doctor and he was finding it uphill work remembering the medical words.

'Words like "cerebellum" and "superior vena cava" fly out of my head like migrating birds,' said poor Joe despairingly. 'Not one of 'em chooses to nest under my thatch. There's a story going round, Mr. Philpott, that you have doses of an instant sort that might help a fellow like me out of his difficulties.'

Mr. Philpott took his favourite blue jar down from the shelf. 'This will help you in more ways than one, Joe,' he cried. 'It's Instant Wisdom. Care to try it?'

Joe Brassbound was willing to trying anything that would help him to remember long words. He took a dose of Instant Wisdom and instantly remembered not only 'cerebellum' and 'superior vena cava' but words like 'electrocardiogram' and 'endoplasmic reticulum' which he hadn't even studied yet. Not only this. He calculated the orbit of the planet Mars and got it right the first time. 'Curious,' thought Mr. Philpott, a little disappointed. This was more like cleverness than wisdom, but only time would tell. Joe himself was so delighted that he promptly bought a big carton of honey, a packet of peppermints, some lean bacon and two tins of baked beans, a very satisfactory sale for Mr. Philpott.

Then there was another, prolonged rush on Instant Beauty for both men and women and a good sale of pink hand-mirrors which Mr. Philpott had optimistically put out as 'specials' that very morning, and then a dose of Instant Youth for old Mrs. Soames who was eighty-seven and so bent over with her years that it was a wonder she didn't choose to throw her sticks away and roll along like a hoop. As it was she went skipping out of the shop aged about seventeen, and pushing a shopping trolley filled with 'Zooosh the Wonder Cleaner' and fourteen boxes of pancake mix. When she had been seventeen the first time round, seventy years earlier, she had enjoyed pancakes more than anything else in the world and now she was really looking forward to enjoying them again.

Next Mr. Philpott was gratified to have Mr. Carnelian the Mayor as a customer. The Mayor was well known for opening car parks and by-passes with very boring speeches. Now he sidled in pretending he'd come for soda water, and went out successfully dosed with Instant Wit. That evening, at a small civic ceremony, he gave a speech so funny that all who heard it declared they'd sooner watch the Mayor open the new civic pensioners' flats than watch a three-ring circus on television. It was all quite exciting. Not only was the ordinary humdrum town being transformed by Beauty, Wit, Strength, Courage and Wisdom but sales at the corner grocery rocketed to an all-time high. The following day there was another early morning queue outside the corner grocery and Mr. Philpott looked anxiously at his supplies of the Domdaniel Instants, now getting rather low, particularly Instant Wisdom—which was strange as very few people had yet asked for it. But Mr Philpott needn't have worried, for on the third day the Traveller was back in town checking on the sales of Domdaniel Instants and talking to the many, many people who had tried them out.

7 Nobody Listens to the Traveller

There was something puzzled and even desperate about the Traveller as he wandered around studying the townspeople and trying to get their attention.

'King of the World?' Damian Bullock looked polite but surprised. 'I haven't time for that. Copper and I are inventing rocket-powered roller skates. I'll think about being king when the skates are finished.'

'Queen of the World?' Mrs. Soames exclaimed. 'At my age?'

'You look a mere seventeen and wonderfully beautiful into the bargain. You could be rich and powerful as well,' the Traveller wheedled.

'But at present I'm working on a revolutionary new pancake mix,' Mrs. Soames said. 'And I'm planning to get into the *Guinness Book of Records* for eating more pancakes than anyone has ever eaten before. It's a full enough life as it is without royal ambitions.'

'But if you were Queen you could have all the pancakes you wanted without having to go to the trouble of making them,' the Traveller pointed out.

'But making them is half the fun,' Mrs. Soames explained. Her eyes became suddenly sharp. 'Wait a minute—who are you? Haven't I met you before?'

'Not recently,' the Traveller mumbled. 'Maybe a few years ago . . .'

'I'm too old to be taken in by YOU,' Mrs. Soames exclaimed.

'But you're only seventeen,' the Traveller reminded her slyly.

'Funny—that,' Mrs. Soames looked pensive. 'I thought I *was* seventeen but perhaps you never really can be seventeen again—even with Instant Youth. I'll cook you a pancake if you like, but any more of that Queen of the World talk and I'll hit you with the frying pan. I'm just not interested, and that's all there is to it.'

* * *

'Mr. Brassbound—the CLEVER Mr. Brassbound?' asked the Traveller, rising unexpectedly out of a bed of geraniums and sidling up to Joe Brassbound.

'I'm no cleverer than anyone else in town,' answered Joe looking surprised.

'Oh, I'm much more impressed with you than with the others,' the Traveller said quickly and Joe looked pleased.

'I'm very good at orbits now,' he said. 'I can do Mars and Jupiter and even Pluto and Halley's comet.'

'That's all very well,' the Traveller objected, 'but don't you ever think of putting your abilities to some use? You could make others obey you, you could be powerful. You could have servants to supply your merest wishes.'

Joe gave the Traveller a glance as clear as air, calm and gentle, yet somehow terrifying to the Traveller who hissed like a cat and turned away from Joe as if from a bright light.

'I don't want to have anyone obeying me,' Joe said. 'I'm calculating the hardest orbit of them all, Mr. Traveller, and that's my own orbit. I don't know quite what it is yet, but it won't make me powerful—I can tell you that. And Mr. Traveller . . . there's a tail with a point on it hanging down below your coat '

Looking very angry, but with his tail curled up out of sight, the Traveller decided to call on Mr. Philpott at the corner grocery. Mr. Philpott was extremely busy, serving grateful customers. The Traveller had to wait quite a while to speak to him alone.

'Our pilot scheme seems to be going like a bomb!' the Traveller said, and Mr. Philpott agreed with him.

'But you don't seem to have tried any of them yourself,' the Traveller went on uneasily.

'No!' said Mr. Philpott. 'I'm happy as I am, particularly now that trade's improved a bit.' The Traveller looked highly discontented.

'We'll see!' he said at last. 'Early days yet,' and minced out on his strange feet, smiling horribly over his shoulder at Mr

Philpott as he went. Mr. Philpott knew he had locked the door that the Traveller opened so easily. He checked it, and it *was* locked, no mistake about that.

'Dear me!' Mr. Philpott sighed. 'He thinks I'm a fool, and perhaps I am. But a man as old as I am . . . well, I've caught sight of that Traveller and his kind on and off for years. As if I couldn't recognize one of them when I meet one face to face.' His grumblings were interrupted by a sudden change of light by the rack of seed packets and he looked over to see what had caused it.

The golden-eyed Stranger stood there watching him doubtfully.

'Good evening,' he said, and his voice resounded among the dry goods and groceries. 'It's an interesting town these days,' the man went on. 'As I went past the town garage I saw two incredibly handsome young men holding a car up in the air, one at each end, while another fixed its exhaust system and they were arguing about the reasons for the disappearance of the dinosaurs. Unusual I thought.'

'I don't know,' said Mr. Philpott. 'It *is* interesting. I often wonder about it myself.'

'But they were speaking in Ancient Greek. Three young men all speaking about dinosaurs in Ancient Greek! That must be unusual.'

'We're getting used to it around here,' Mr. Philpott explained apologetically. 'There's been a lot of that sort of thing going on over the last day or two.'

'I hope you realize what you're doing,' the Stranger said sternly to Mr. Philpott. 'Suppose the very talented people of this very talented town find the town too small for their talents? Suppose they decide that they want to be Kings and Queens of the World?'

'Then I'd be Grocer by Royal Appointment, I suppose,' said Mr. Philpott, grinning a bit. 'But don't you worry . . . they're very sensible people in this neck of the woods. I can promise you that.'

'I hope they are,' replied the Stranger grimly.

127

'Hope, hope, hope!' echoed the tins of tomato soup and spaghetti on their shelves.

'Have more faith in your product!' Mr. Philpott shouted after him. 'Beauty, courage, wisdom. . . .' he added to himself as the door slammed. 'All good things! Doesn't he realize that Domdaniel Productions made a mistake in the first place. And doesn't he realize I've been corner grocer here for thirty-five years and I know a hawk from a handsaw. The people in this town are a sensible lot. Up and down they go, to and fro, this way and that . . . but deep down they're level-headed, I'm sure of it.'

He spoke aloud to the locked door, but the pie-dishes, nutmeg graters, and tins of tomato soup sat silent on their shelves as if refusing to agree with him.

8 *The Evening of the Party*

Within a week or so Mr. Philpott's town became the most remarkable town in the world. It was like living in the heart of a carnival—a beautiful circus where everyone was clown, tight-rope walker, strongman and bareback rider all rolled into one. At first Instant Beauty and Instant Strength were the most popular among the Domdaniel Instants, but then Instant Wisdom started to move forward. People wore flowers in their hair and used their new skill to make themselves wonderful clothes, printed with flowers, cobwebs, notes of music, golden beetles, snowflakes, peacock feathers, shivery grasses, new moons and green smiling lions.

Never before had the walls echoed such wise conversations, such happy laughter. Up in her room Mrs. Soames made delicious pancakes and invited everybody to breakfast. When breakfast was over everyone went to school, even the mothers and fathers and babies and grandparents, which was rather strange because they all knew as much as the teachers, thanks to Instant Wisdom. But there always turned out to be someone

who knew more about something than other people did and part of the fun of school was finding out whose turn it was to do the knowing for that day.

There were concerts held on the beach where everybody played and sang, and there were sports days when everybody raced and jumped. It was nothing for sprinters to run a kilometre in less than two minutes or for jumpers to use their new super-strength to jump five metres high. The library had never had such a busy time. At first it issued a lot of books—so many books that the shelves were totally empty—but then everyone in town took to writing books of poetry and history and science and the shelves filled up again. The town had never had an art gallery, but now so many people painted marvellous pictures that it had to have one.

And in the middle of town in his corner shop Mr. Philpott sold sticking plaster, apple juice, cotton wool, baking powder, mixing spoons, cinnamon, macaroni, dishmops, envelopes and all the other useful household things . . . but surprisingly few people were now asking for the Domdaniel Instants. Mr. Philpott watched the town carefully over the top of his spectacles.

'So far, so good,' he muttered.

9 *Magic at Midnight*

But the Traveller was not pleased.

'Well, well,' he began cheerfully enough on his next visit to the corner shop. 'Things are a bit slow again, aren't they? We have a new line of Instants as well as the same old replacements for you. Look! Instant Greed! That should give a boost to food sales. Instant Anger—that's very useful for getting your own way, you know, and Instant Pride to give people a proper view of themselves. I didn't bring them before—they're a bit ahead of their time—but since the others have done so well . . .'

'Oh, I can't see any of those lines being successful,' Mr Philpott said. 'As I said, business has dropped off in some o' he Instants. Instant Beauty has declined a bit and so has Instant Strength . . . even Instant Youth . . . and people aren't coming back for booster doses. The novelty's worn off, I suppose.'

The Traveller's dark blush swept his face again. His thin lips curled back showing a mouthful of teeth like needles and a tongue like a blue flame, flickering behind them.

'I'm not very happy with the way you're marketing these goods,' he cried. 'I'd have expected a lot more consumer reaction, quite frankly. They've got Instant Beauty, they've got Instant Cleverness.'

'Wisdom,' Mr. Philpott corrected him.

'Same thing,' the Traveller snarled. 'Why are they happy to stay here in this tin-pot town when they could be out tearing the world to bits? You've gone about things in the wrong way and I'm going to have to promote this line through the supermarkets after all.'

Mr. Philpott coughed tactfully. 'The supermarket has closed down,' he said. 'Well, they needed an art gallery so badly. Now there's no use taking it so hard. I just don't need to reorder. Stock is holding out very well.'

The Traveller gave Mr. Philpott the look of one who has taken an immense dose of Instant Malice. 'And what about you, you silly old grocer?' he hissed. 'Why don't you try something yourself . . . Instant Beauty, say?'

'I'm beautiful enough,' said Mr. Philpott. 'Ask anyone.'

'Instant Youth?' persisted the Traveller. His eyes were blazing and a thin thread of smoke was escaping at the corner of his mouth.

'I just don't want to go through all that again,' said Mr. Philpott shaking his head. 'Once was quite enough.'

'Instant Cleverness?' hissed the Traveller coming so close that Mr. Philpott could smell the scorching gun-powdery smell of his breath and feel heat coming off him as it does off a wood stove.

'I'm clever enough for most and too clever for some,' said Mr. Philpott sternly. 'And I must remind you.' He pointed to a polite notice on his counter. 'No smoking in this shop, please.' For smoke had begun to pour from the Traveller's mouth and nose and ears while his eyes blazed through his own haze with a fearful longing.

'I'll be back again!' he shouted. 'Fourth time pays for all!' He ran out on to the footpath and vanished like a burst bubble.

'He'll be back!' said a voice that rang among the jam-pots and pie-dishes—and there stood the hunchbacked Stranger.

Mr. Philpott gazed after the Traveller and spoke reflectively.

'He gave me this,' (picking up his blue jar). 'Said I couldn't go wrong. And he doesn't understand why things aren't working out for him. He called it Instant Cleverness, did you notice? Doesn't he realize there's a difference between cleverness and wisdom?'

'Perhaps he doesn't,' said the Stranger. 'When he does realize, there will be instant anger.'

'He thinks his Instants did it all,' went on Mr. Philpott. 'Well, of course they helped people to realize they were halfway there already, you know. They were half wise, half brave, half strong, and half beautiful. Half greedy, too, of course, half angry as well! I'd never agree to sell Instants of that sort even to compete with the supermarket.'

'Be careful!' said the Stranger. 'Pride, even if you're only half proud, goes before a fall.'

'I can manage,' said Mr. Philpott obstinately.

The Stranger stepped through the grocery door and vanished like a blown-out candle.

'Coming and going! Coming and going! Very restless fellows, both of them,' muttered Mr. Philpott.

Then he shut the shop, put on his best clothes and went to a party in the civic park where people sang and recited poems they had written, read from their books and painted pictures. Everyone was wise and beautiful and witty and brave except, it seemed, he himself, Jack Philpott, who was watching them over his spectacles. As midnight came they took hands and formed circles, one circle dancing inside another. Slowly they

132

egan to turn in a spinning dance and to sing very quietly a soft
ild song so powerful that Mr. Philpott felt the season change
round him. Mr. Philpott thought the ring of dancers had
ecome a wheel of stars and expected to see them rise from the
arth and disappear spinning and singing into space. Instead
omething else happened.

The song ended, the dance ended and a great silence fell on
e people, a deep serene stillness, as if in the very moment of
eir being all together, each one of them had also become
ompletely alone. Then they turned to each other with the
leased, surprised looks of people who have guessed the answer
 a very difficult riddle. They let their hands drop and moved
way from their circle like birds flying home, like leaves falling
 autumn. Something magical had happened, something had
een completed. Mr. Philpott could not tell quite what had
appened for he was the only person in town who had not taken
 dose of the Domdaniel Instants.

But it did not make as much difference as you might
uppose.

10 *A Drop in Sales*

he silence stayed over the town like a gentle dream for three
ays and then the town began to change again. The change
egan with Joe Brassbound.

'Come for your booster dose of Wisdom?' Mr. Philpott
sked Joe as he came through the door.

'Fact is,' said Joe, giving Mr. Philpott an anxious glance, 'it
n't that I'm not grateful, Mr. Philpott, but I thought I'd go
ithout. I just looked in to buy condensed milk and some
atmeal.'

'What! Do you think you'll pass your next exams without a
ose of Instant Wisdom, Joe?' demanded Mr Philpott.

'Not a chance!' said Joe almost cheerfully, 'but you see Mr.
hilpott, that Instant Wisdom worked strangely in a way.

What I mean is that I calculated the orbit of the planet Ma
straight off after I took the first dose. Well, it helped m
calculate my own orbit too, as it were, and I found I didn
want to be a doctor whether I could pass the exams or not. S
now I'm going out of town to work on my friend's farm. I'
always wanted to be a farmer but I didn't realize it un
Instant Wisdom set me to calculating orbits and working ov
the rotations of my dreams.'

'Well, Joe, that's all very well, but you have to be wise to l
a farmer,' Mr. Philpott said. 'It's not easy, you know.'

'I know that,' Joe agreed, 'but I'm already wise in the rig
way for farming and what I don't know I'll learn without ar
more doses.' Smiling, he added, 'Instant Wisdom's like su
denly arriving at an exciting place without rememberir
anything of the journey, although you know the journey mu
have been more exciting still. What Instant Wisdom ende
up by saying to me was "Back to the beginning, Joe. No
you know where you're going you have to take the long wa
round".'

'I see,' said Mr. Philpott, who really did see a long way ove
the top of his glasses.

'And besides,' said Joe, 'there's my girlfriend, Sally, M
Philpott. She lives in another town and—well, she's got to tak
the long way round, so I'm going with her, you see. No mor
Instant Wisdoms for me, but I will have that condensed mil
and the oatmeal, and a block of cheese just to show there are n
hard feelings.'

Curiously enough Joe was not the only person who came i
that day and bought groceries but turned down his dose of th
Domdaniel Instants. Mrs. Soames, for instance, not only gav
up Beauty but Youth too.

'Let's face it, Jack,' she said, 'I've grown wise enough t
know I'm eighty-seven *here*.' She placed her hand on her hear
'I've worked hard all my life to get to eighty-seven and sud
denly I want to see what eighty-eight's like—and I've ha
enough pancakes to last me until I'm a hundred. So no mor
Instant Youth, Jack, but give me a packet of tea and some o

134

hose nice chocolate biscuits. I love chocolate biscuits with my tea, even first thing in the morning when I know I shouldn't.'

People began to drift back to what they had been in the days before the Domdaniel Instants, though somehow they were not quite the same people. Something of the Instant magic remained with them, becoming less and less Instant and more and more part of their everyday selves as the days went by.

Damian and Copper Candle, good friends now, gave up Super Strength because it took a lot of the fun out of weight lifting. Alona Perry came into the shop arm in arm with young Jack Thingummy from down the road.

'I've got a leading part in a play,' she told Mr. Philpott triumphantly. 'I'm a heroine at last.'

'You'll want a drop more Instant Beauty, then!' Mr. Philpott reached for his lavender-coloured jar. Alona laughed.

'Would you believe it,' she said, 'I nearly missed the part because I was too pretty for it. I've got to get my freckles back again.'

'And I want her to have her old nose, too,' said Jack. 'I liked that old nose, particularly the bump on it. I think a straight nose is as boring as a straight road, don't you, Mr. Philpott?'

'But,' said Alona, 'we will have dried fruit, golden syrup, a dozen eggs, a pound of butter, a tin of crushed pineapple, almonds, walnuts, candied peel, crystallized cherries and two packets of icing sugar. I made my wedding dress last week and now we're going to make a wedding cake together. Everyone's invited and there will be dancing and fireworks.'

'It's a pleasure, Alona,' said Mr. Philpott beaming. 'I think fireworks make a lovely wedding, but my word, the Domdaniel Instants are looking a bit on the dusty side. Perhaps I'll sell a few more doses tomorrow.'

But he didn't, nor the day after that. The market for Domdaniel Instants had faded away.

10 *The Traveller Is Very Angry*

Friday evening was late opening night and Mr. Philpott kept his door open. He ate two ham sandwiches with rather a lot of mustard and drank two cups of very strong tea during the quiet time of evening when everyone else was having dinner and making long lists of useful groceries they would need for the weekend.

The little grocery was warm with its hissing heater and yellow electric lights yet suddenly the lights dimmed threateningly while the heater went dark and silent. The corner grocery became as cold as a wicked wish. Mr. Philpott knew who was there without looking up, and he sighed to himself as he lifted his eyes and stared sternly over his spectacles. The Traveller stood before him, meeting his gaze with a savage smile. It was as if he had slashed at him with a razor of ice. Mr. Philpott felt his joints begin to freeze at that smile.

'Business good?' asked the Traveller.

'Well . . .' Mr. Philpott began and made his stiff, cold lips smile back. The Traveller shrank a little before the smile, but recovered quickly. He put a jar on the counter . . . a jar filled with a sullen black powder shifting and oozing behind the glass like angry mud. 'Instant Hate!' he said. 'Sell this, and we'll say no more about your bad sales of the other Instants.'

'I certainly shall not,' Mr. Philpott said, and felt the cold bite into him.

'I've been around town,' the Traveller went on, 'and—I don't know what's happened, but you've wrecked everything, you stupid old fool. People are giving up their powers, surrendering Beauty, signing off from Super-strength, sundering themselves from Cleverness. It should have been the sell-out of the century. Years of marketing research have gone into this programme. Somehow you've ruined it all and I mean to get even with you. You'll be sorry you ever were born when I've finished with you.'

'You're wrong,' Mr. Philpott managed to whisper. He was almost paralysed with cold. 'People here have become wise

nough to discover their true beauty, and are brave and strong
nough to be content with themselves. Your Instants were
ood fun . . . but they aren't needed any more, that's all.'

'Fun? Fun?' screamed the Traveller. 'That's all, you say. It
AN'T be all. You are to blame for this.'

'Not me,' replied Mr. Philpott. 'You are to blame because
ou confused wisdom with mere cleverness. You meant to
nake people slick and smart but you made them wise by
nistake.'

'Cleverness! Wisdom! It's the same thing,' the Traveller
narled.

Mr. Philpott actually managed a little frozen chuckle and
eemed to get a little warmer as he went on. 'You may be clever
nough in your way but you're certainly not wise. Cleverness
night wear off in ten days, but not wisdom, not ever. Wisdom
hanges the brain, reveals hidden passages and wonderful
vinding journeys, opens doors to lost libraries, unexpected art
alleries and observatories, flings wide windows on to streets
lled with clowns and carnivals and comets. That's what wis-
om does. Fancy you giving me Instant Wisdom. You silly
lemon, I've been putting a little Instant Wisdom into every
lose I've given to anybody in this shop ever since I realized
our mistake.'

The Traveller began to smoke at hearing this long speech.
Mr. Philpott felt suddenly terrified at the shafts of anger and
lestruction that came darting at him.

'Well, much good may it do you,' the creature cried.
mmediately he changed. Before Mr. Philpott stood his very
wn reflection, a Mr. Philpott complete to his short nose and
is spectacles sliding down it. Only the gleaming eyes looking
ver the glasses were different from his own, and they boiled
nd bubbled with fury. And the more heated he became
he colder Mr. Philpott grew, until he felt frozen to the
narrow.

'It's time the grocery had a new grocer,' said the Traveller,
he words steaming and spitting on his burning lips. 'I shall tear
ou to pieces, you ugly, stupid, cowardly old man—pieces so

137

small that the very worms will need glasses in order to find them. I shall sell Instant Hate and Instant Cruelty among the other Domdaniel Instants so that your silly customers will become beautiful and clever and strong and cruel, kings and queens of the world, greedy for power. You have spoiled my joke, so I shall take your place.'

'They won't buy anything from you,' Mr. Philpott said with a tremendous effort. 'Take a dose of Instant Despair and give in!'

'They won't know the difference,' cried the Traveller, unable to stop smoking just a little bit at his nose.

'Yes, we will!' cried other voices.

There in the doorway of the shop were clustered a group of Mr. Philpott's corner grocery customers, who had come to buy and stayed to listen.

'Leave him alone or I'll knock you down!' said Damian bravely.

'Lay a hand on him and you'll have me to reckon with!' shouted Mrs. Soames in a young voice, skipping like a pancake on a hot pan.

'Don't you dare touch him,' cried Alona, beautiful as a goddess in her defiance.

'He'll be too much for you, one way or another,' murmured Joe Brassbound wisely.

'Well and good!' sneered the Traveller, 'I shall tear him to bits before your eyes and then take my Domdaniel Instants to another town.'

'One minute . . .' said Mr. Philpott, though his lips could barely move now with the terrible chill that held him in its hard embrace. 'I acknowledge I can't manage any more, and I ask to speak to the rival firm.'

'The rival firm?' shrieked the Traveller, falling back smoking and writhing. He made a move to strike Mr. Philpott dumb, which he would have done earlier had he had been wiser, but Mr. Philpott had already spoken.

'Paradise Enterprises,' he whispered, and felt his bones, very faintly, begin to grow warm again.

The air turned golden and the whole corner grocery began a melodious hum as if it were filled with a swarm of invisible bees.

12 Down through the Floor and up through the Ceiling

The Stranger appeared, stranger no longer. He was not wearing his white business suit but a white robe and silver sandals. His hair shivered in the air like blue smoke, his eyes burned gold. From his shoulders, free at last, sprang two great feathery wings, as white as snow, the big quills edged with scarlet and gold. The Traveller let out a terrible shriek.

'Dealing with the opposition!' He showed his needle teeth. 'Where's integrity in business these shallow days? I'll always go to the supermarkets after this!' With a click he changed from Mr. Philpott's shape to his Traveller's shape and then to another, older shape, all claws and hoofs and horns and a turning pointed tail. He made a stabbing gesture at Mr. Philpott with a pitchfork that had mysteriously appeared in his hairy hands.

'Avaunt Belial!' said the Stranger . . . giving the Traveller one of his many true names. The Traveller shrieked and stamped with his hoofs upon the corner grocery floor which conveniently split open for him. Smoke and fire poured out scorching the front of the counter and turning all the shortbread in a wire display-rack brown. Then the floor closed again. The Traveller was gone.

There was a cheer from the shop doorway.

'Three cheers for our corner grocer!' cried young Jack.

'He couldn't be braver,' declared Damian.

'Or wiser!' Joe Brassbound added.

'Or more beautiful!' Alona said, smiling and crying all at once.

'Business as usual on Monday,' replied Mr. Philpott looking

139

fondly at them all, and then rather gloomily at his scorche[d] counter. 'This shortbread will be a "Special" and there will [be] free apples for anyone who buys oatmeal or wholemeal brea[d.] Thanks for your patronage and I hope I may count upon yo[ur] continued support in the future.'

There was more cheering as he firmly locked his door f[or] the night. It had been a full evening.

'You did need me after all,' said the Stranger.

'Do what you can yourself, and *then* call in the experts,' M[r.] Philpott said. 'That's my policy. You can take the Domdan[ic] Instants with you now. There's no more demand, you see, a[nd] I'll need that space for instant soups.'

'You did very well, really,' said the Stranger. 'Better than [I] thought you would.'

'I expect you get a bit pessimistic at times, in your line [of] work,' Mr. Philpott said sympathetically. 'But I told you . . . have more faith in the product.' He passed the Stranger h[is] favourite Instant . . . the blue one.

'Wisdom?' asked the Stranger reading the label.

'Faith in people too!' Mr. Philpott added seriously.

The Stranger smiled for the first time, and the air arou[nd] him shone and smelt of honey. Every grocery in the shop sa[ng] in its own true voice so that the humming changed into a glass[y,] tinny, rustling, ringing music. The smile was so dazzling th[at] Mr. Philpott had to look away and it was only out of the ve[ry] corner of his eye that he saw the ceiling open and the Strang[er] take off on his great wings, sailing up and out into a dark bl[ue] sky freckled with stars. His flight filled the shop with a war[m,] honey-scented hurricane that blew paper-bags and envelop[es] and jam-pot covers and instant soup all over the floor. As he le[ft] his silver sandal knocked over a shelf of baking powder, pr[e-] served ginger and various spices.

Mr. Philpott swore in a small way, and then looked u[p] anxiously. His ceiling had closed again perfectly. Slowly [he] smiled his own smile, not a thin smile and not a dazzling one[.]

'I'll pick them up tomorrow,' he said. 'It's been a long day[.'] And then he thought, 'I'll have another cup of tea and do

140

now. God knows what tomorrow's got in store,' and he nodded in a friendly fashion at his own ceiling.

'I'm glad I'm a corner grocer,' he mused as he put the kettle on. 'You meet all sorts in this business,' and the groceries seemed to stir on their shelves as if they agreed.

Also available from Mammoth

Also by Margaret Mahy

THE HAUNTING

'When, suddenly, on an ordinary Wednesday, it seemed to Barney that the world tilted and ran downhill in all directions, he knew he was about to be haunted again.'

Tabitha can't help noticing the change in Barney – how quiet he's become, his pale expression and those dazed eyes which seem to be seeing things from another world. But as Tabitha determines to solve the mystery she finds herself in very deep waters. Who *was* Barney's Great-Uncle Cole? Is he really dead? And who can save Barney from the terrifying experiences which seem to be taking hold of him?

'Strong and terrifying . . . The novel winds up like a spring. A psychological thriller.'
Times Literary Supplement

'A generous humour tempers the eerie thrills of this ingenious story.'
Naomi Lewis, *The Observer*

'Supernatural happenings and psychic powers, all packed into a ghost story that holds us until the last page is turned.' *New York Times Book Review*

Eric Morecambe

THE RELUCTANT VAMPIRE

With illustrations by Tony Ross

'I don't like blood. I like chips and a small glass of red wine.' The Vampire Prince's shocking announcement begins a fantastic tale of ghoulish intrigue, spooky spells and hilarious horror!

'Slapstick dialogue and ghoulish goings-on . . .'
The Mail on Sunday

'Sparkling and spooky ... full of wit and word-play.' *Lancashire Evening Post*

A Selected List of Fiction from Mammoth

While every effort is made to keep prices low, it is sometimes necessary to increase prices at short notice. Mammoth Books reserves the right to show new retail prices on covers which may differ from those previously advertised in the text or elsewhere.

The prices shown below were correct at the time of going to press.

☐	416 13972 8	**Why the Whales Came**	Michael Murpurgo	£2.50
☐	7497 0034 3	**My Friend Walter**	Michael Murpurgo	£2.50
☐	7497 0035 1	**The Animals of Farthing Wood**	Colin Dann	£2.99
☐	7497 0136 6	**I Am David**	Anne Holm	£2.50
☐	7497 0139 0	**Snow Spider**	Jenny Nimmo	£2.50
☐	7497 0140 4	**Emlyn's Moon**	Jenny Nimmo	£2.25
☐	7497 0344 X	**The Haunting**	Margaret Mahy	£2.25
☐	416 96850 3	**Catalogue of the Universe**	Margaret Mahy	£1.95
☐	7497 0051 3	**My Friend Flicka**	Mary O'Hara	£2.99
☐	7497 0079 3	**Thunderhead**	Mary O'Hara	£2.99
☐	7497 0219 2	**Green Grass of Wyoming**	Mary O'Hara	£2.99
☐	416 13722 9	**Rival Games**	Michael Hardcastle	£1.99
☐	416 13212 X	**Mascot**	Michael Hardcastle	£1.99
☐	7497 0126 9	**Half a Team**	Michael Hardcastle	£1.99
☐	416 08812 0	**The Whipping Boy**	Sid Fleischman	£1.99
☐	7497 0033 5	**The Lives of Christopher Chant**	Diana Wynne-Jones	£2.50
☐	7497 0164 1	**A Visit to Folly Castle**	Nina Beechcroft	£2.25

All these books are available at your bookshop or newsagent, or can be ordered direct from the publisher. Just tick the titles you want and fill in the form below.

Mandarin Paperbacks, Cash Sales Department, PO Box 11, Falmouth, Cornwall TR10 9EN.

Please send cheque or postal order, no currency, for purchase price quoted and allow the following for postage and packing:

UK   80p for the first book, 20p for each additional book ordered to a maximum charge of £2.00.

BFPO   80p for the first book, 20p for each additional book.

Overseas   £1.50 for the first book, £1.00 for the second and 30p for each additional book
including Eire   thereafter.

NAME (Block letters) ....

ADDRESS ....

....

....